I0780087

ELLEN FANNON

Dogged By Murder

By Ellen Fannon

ISBN-13: 978-1-965352-83-0

ALSO BY ELLEN FANNON

Other People's Children
Save the Date – 2022 Christian Indie Award winner
Don't Bite the Doctor
Honor Thy Father – Episode One
Honor Thy Father —Episode Two

LOVE IN THE WIND SERIES

Love in the Wind —Book One —2024 Living Water Award Winner
Falling For a Cowboy – Book Two
Loves' Trail of Redemption —Book Three

Chapter One

"*Where* is Dr. Collins?" The plump, well-endowed older woman glared at me from behind spectacles perched on the bridge of her patrician nose. Nestled in her ample bosom, a tiny Apple Head Chihuahua peeked out, its bulging eyes wide with terror.

Why was it always the biggest owners who had the smallest dogs?

"Dr. Collins is in the emergency room with a kidney stone," I said. "I'm filling in for him. I'm Dr. Amy Dixon."

I extended my hand. She looked at it as if I'd insulted her dog's pedigree. "In the emergency room?" she shrieked—well, as much as her booming voice could shriek. "That's unacceptable!"

Not quite sure I'd heard her correctly, I said, "Excuse me?"

"I *said*, young lady, that's unacceptable. I must see him at once. Evangelina Rose has an emergency."

"Um . . . who is Evangelina Rose?"

The woman's lips thinned to nothing before her eyes bugged out, mirroring her dog's. "Evangelina Rose is my dog," she said icily. "My *champion* show dog, as Dr. Collins well knows."

I glanced at the quivering creature burrowing deeper into her owner's cleavage. "Perhaps if you tell me what's wrong, I can help."

The woman's nostrils flared. "Absolutely not! Evangelina Rose only sees Dr. Collins."

"As I've already explained, Ms. . . . ."

"Blankenship. *Mrs.* Mildred Blankenship. And I insist you call Dr. Collins *immediately.*"

I blinked. "I'm not sure you understand, Mrs. Blankenship. Dr. Collins is in the—"

"Yes, yes, I heard you." She waved a dismissive hand. "Just tell him Evangelina Rose needs him, and he'll come. He can take some Tylenol or morphine or *something.*"

We had a stare-down. I looked away first. "I'm afraid I can't do that."

If looks could kill, I'd be a corpse. "Now you listen to me, Missy." She punctuated each word with a sharp jab of her index finger, barely missing my chest. Evangelina Rose tremored so violently that it looked as though her owner was doing "the shimmy."

"You *will* call him this minute, or I'll report you to the veterinary medical board—if you're even a real veterinarian."

Her face flushed a dangerous shade of red. For a moment, I worried she'd have a stroke and end up in the emergency room with Dr. Collins. But at least then she'd get to see him, though probably without Evangelina Rose.

Enough was enough. Although I'd only been in practice for a few years, I'd seen my fair share of bullies. And I wasn't about to be steamrolled by Mildred Blankenship.

"No," I said calmly.

Her jaw clenched so tightly I thought she might crack a molar. A blood vessel in her temple pulsed, and I feared it would rupture and spray me with her venomous blood. She sucked in a sharp breath, forcing Evangelina Rose further into the recess of her bosom. "We'll just see about this! I'm going to Mr. Wigglesworth, the show organizer, and have you fired. *Then* I'll report you for malpractice!"

She spun on her heel and stomped away across the concrete floor, her footfalls sending the group of Jack Russell Terriers parading around the ring opposite the veterinary first aid station into a frenzy. But, to be fair, it didn't take much to send Jack Russells into a frenzy.

"What was *that* all about?" I turned to see a gorgeous young man in a red apron standing at my elbow. He had warm brown eyes and a crooked grin, which made my heart do a flip-flop.

I shrugged. "Apparently, I'm not Dr. Collins."

He chuckled. "Yeah, I can see that. You're a lot better looking than he is."

My face warmed. "Not to Mrs. Blankenship, I'm not."

He snorted. "Don't let her get to you. Everyone around here calls her Mrs. Battleship."

A giggle escaped my lips. "I guess that about sums her up."

"Though I've never seen Mr. Battleship. Either he's a figment of her imagination, or she sank him a long time ago." His eyes glinted with mischief. Sticking out his hand, he said, "I'm Nick. Nick Wyman."

I shook it. "It's nice to meet you, Nick Wyman. I'm Amy Dixon." Firm, masculine grip. I hung on just a fraction too long as I gazed into his exquisite eyes. "So, I take it you've worked a lot of dog shows?"

"My family has the concessions contract. I've been around the dog show circuit since I was in kindergarten." He flashed a grin—straight white teeth, the kind that probably didn't come cheap. "I'm just filling in today since I'm off work. In real life, I'm an insurance adjuster at Crosby and Kessler."

I briefly questioned the wisdom of placing the medical station next to the snack bar, but I wasn't in charge of the Claymore County Dog Show. I was only here because of the frantic phone call from Dr. Collins' wife early this morning.

"Insurance adjuster *and* hot dog vendor. I'm impressed."

"Yeah, I make a mean bag of popcorn, too." He looked over my shoulder and uttered, "Uh-oh."

"What?" I twisted around to see Mildred Battleship . . . er, Blankenship gesticulating wildly to a small, skinny, bald man wearing an official blue vest. Evangelina Rose had disappeared altogether. The man glanced my way and frowned.

"The old battle-ax is reaming out Mr. Wigglesworth, the show organizer. You'll notice by the way he's standing that he has no spine."

My spine stiffened as the two marched back to where we stood.

"What's this about you refusing to help Mrs. Blankenship's dog?" the man demanded in a less-than-masculine voice.

"I did no such thing." I cast what I hoped was a withering look at the woman. "I am more than happy to take care of whatever problem Evangelina Rose has, which, I might add, Mrs. Blankenship refuses to tell me."

"The name's bigger than the dog," Nick muttered under his breath.

Mr. Wigglesworth turned back to an angry Mrs. Blankenship. "Just what is the problem with your dog?"

She pursed her lips. Then, after heaving a dramatic sigh, she said, "Evangelina Rose has torn a toenail."

Okay, now *my* eyes bugged out like the dog's. *A torn toenail*? Seriously?

Mr. Wigglesworth fixed an intimidating stare on me. Or, I guessed it was meant to be intimidating. It fell rather short of the mark. "I demand you take care of this problem immediately."

As tempting as it was to tell the man to find another veterinarian to take the abuse from unreasonable owners at the dog show—and, yeah, good luck with that, by the way—I *had* promised Dr. Collins' wife I'd take care of everything. I bit my tongue. Literally. Maybe, with any luck, Dr. Collins would pass that stone and be back in an hour or so, morphine-induced haze and all.

Nick stood by, his eyes darting among the three of us. Apparently, no one needed a hot dog at the moment. But I did notice a small crowd gathering on the periphery, evidently drawn in by the unfolding drama.

Without a word, I reached toward Mrs. Blankenship's heaving bosom. "If you'll hand me Evangelina Rose, please."

Seeing that she had no choice, Mrs. Blankenship reached into the nether regions of her anatomy that I tried valiantly not to imagine and extracted the dog. But she still maintained a tight grip on the trembling animal. I did not want to engage in a tug-of-war, so I dropped my hands. She held out one of Evangelina Rose's front paws.

"Right there." She thrust the foot under my nose and isolated the injured nail with her own long, fuchsia talon.

I squinted to see the damage.

"Right *there*!" Her voice rose with impatience. "Can't you see that?" She turned back to Mr. Wigglesworth, who hunched over to inspect the problem. She tucked Evangelina Rose under one arm and placed her other hand on her wide hip. "Honestly, if this *doctor* can't even see what I'm referring to . . . These matters must be attended to properly so they don't get infected."

"Oh, for pity's sake, Mildred!" Before I knew what was happening, a tall, thin woman swooped in and snatched Evangelina Rose from Mrs. Blankenship's grasp.

She trooped off toward the grooming area at a fast clip, Mrs. Blankenship waddling in her trail, yelling, "Stop, Delores!"

I followed the unexpected turn of events, the crowd pressing in behind me. Just as we all reached the grooming station, the tall woman snipped off the broken section of Evangelina Rose's nail and thrust her back into Mrs. Blankenship's arms.

"There! It didn't even bleed. Stop being such a drama queen!"

Mrs. Blankenship's mouth opened and closed several times as she apparently fought for words. She examined the dog's foot closely, then sputtered, "You can't just *lop* off the nail like you're pruning azaleas! If any complications arise from mutilating my show dog, I'll sue you for everything you've got!"

"Go ahead," Delores shot back. "You won't get much."

Mrs. Blankenship eyed the crowd, then walked off without another word.

Mr. Wigglesworth looked momentarily asea, then moved away in the opposite direction.

"Someone needs to sink that old Battleship for good," a man from the crowd said.

"I'm surprised nobody's snuck arsenic into her coffee," said another.

A middle-aged woman with another Apple Head Chihuahua in her arms said, "She cost my Clementine the championship last year by bribing the judges. I swear, if she does it again this year, I'll kill her."

I blinked at the vehemence with which Mrs. Battleship . . . er, Blankenship was disliked. Letting out a long breath, I turned to go back to the veterinary aid station.

"Well, that was anti-climactic," Nick said, matching his step to mine.

I shook my head. "I had no idea what I was getting myself into. I mean, sure, I know people with show dogs can be a bit . . . over the top, but that's to be expected, I suppose."

"You're right. You have no idea."

I smiled at him. "Thankfully, it's just for one day. Then, I can get back to my normal life-and-death situations, like hit-by-cars and bloats."

He glanced at his vendor's counter. "Oops, looks like I have customers. Can I buy you a hot dog later to make up for the bad start you've gotten this morning?"

I laughed. "Sure. And if you sell candy, bring chocolate."

He winked at me, causing a fluttering in the pit of my stomach. "You've got it."

The next hour passed uneventfully, thank goodness. With the day starting out as it did, I had begun to question my pride in always helping out wherever I was needed. Perhaps the Good Lord was chastising me for my pride. As I scrolled through Facebook posts, I caught the movement of a tall woman walking a dog in my peripheral vision. Delores. I probably should thank her for rescuing me from Mrs. Blankenship.

I rose from my seat. "Delores?"

She turned. "Yes?" For a moment, it appeared she didn't recognize me. Then, a soft smile touched her lips as she headed toward me.

"I just wanted to say thank you for getting me out of that confrontation with Mrs. Blankenship." I stuck out my hand, and she grasped it with a strangling squeeze. I guess groomers had to have strong hands.

Delores huffed out a chuckle. "You're welcome. I've been around enough old bats like her to cut through the nonsense and cut to the chase."

I studied her, impressed. Besides her tall, imposing

stature, her face wore the lines of hard work and common sense. Her graying dark hair, cut in a short, practical bob, framed an angular face. Her hands, large and calloused, sported short, unpainted nails—unlike the standard poodle she walked. She had an overall no-nonsense air about her, an aura of someone who had seen it all and took everything in stride. Her dark, well-worn jeans and button-down shirt were functional and unassuming. A faded green apron covered in dog hair and stains hung from her neck and wrapped around her waist. I had the immediate impression of someone who, while taking no guff from people, managed to exude warmth and calmness when interacting with their dogs. I liked her immediately.

"I take it you've worked the dog show circuit for a while," I said.

"Long enough. After a while, nothing fazes you. Not even self-entitled prima donnas like Mildred Blankenship. Although I have to admit, I have entertained fantasies of taking my nail clippers to her tongue."

The poodle tugged on the leash. "Sit!" Delores commanded in a firm voice, and the dog obeyed. "This is your first rodeo?"

I laughed. "Yes, and probably my last. I'm filling in for Dr. Collins, who had the misfortune of having a kidney stone this morning."

She winced. "Ouch. I've had those before. Thought I would die." The poodle whined, and she shot him a look that would melt steel. He quieted immediately. "So, how long have you been a vet?"

"Three years. I own Happy Tails Veterinary Hospital in Grove City."

"Yeah, I know where that is. Nice place." She clapped me on the shoulder. "Anyway, don't let the Mildred Blankenships get you down."

I nodded. "Usually, I don't. But I just couldn't believe how unreasonable she was being."

Delores clucked her tongue. "Yeah, well, you'll see a lot of those around here. Fortunately, there are enough genuinely nice people to offset them." She glanced down at the dog waiting patiently for our conversation to end. "Well, I'd better get Sir William back to his handler before he comes looking for him."

"Handler?"

She rolled her eyes. "If you're rich enough, you don't even have to show your own dogs."

I grinned. "Thanks, Delores, see you around."

Since things were quiet, I decided to stroll around and get the feel of the place. If anyone needed me, they could always page me over the intercom. The dog show hummed with energy—handlers rushing between rings, spectators chattering excitedly, and the occasional bark cutting through the din. Judges in matching blazers and oversized credentials gathered in tight circles, their expressions grave as if deliberating matters of state rather than canine conformation. Around them, breeders fussed over their prized animals with military precision—brushing, spritzing, and adjusting fur to perfection—while nearby, dogs waited impatiently in crates, their yaps echoing across the hall. In the show rings, owners pranced alongside their canine companions, eyes locked on the coveted, colorful ribbons displayed at the judges' tables.

I hadn't wandered far when a sharp voice sliced through the ambient noise. "Three thousand dollars for a dog I can't breed, and you won't even return my calls? This is unconscionable!"

I froze mid-step, then almost tucked my tail and ran when I saw who the angry woman was addressing. Mrs. Blankenship. But fortunately, she didn't appear to notice me. Nor did she appear to take much notice of the young brunette woman with tightly compressed lips looming over her as she sat calmly grooming a long-haired Chihuahua on a portable table. Mrs. Blankenship's hands never faltered in their rhythmic brushing as if the confrontation were merely background noise.

"What exactly are you talking about, Trudy?" Mrs. Blankenship asked, her voice dripping with boredom as she teased out a tangle in the dog's silky coat.

Trudy planted both hands on her hips, her knuckles whitening. "That dog you sold me—Bentley—has an open fontanelle and hydrocephalus."

Mrs. Blankenship's eyebrow arched delicately, but her attention remained fixed on the tiny dog before her. "That's hardly unusual in Apple Head Chihuahuas. Rarely causes any real issues."

"Rarely? Well, it *has* caused problems." Trudy's voice escalated, drawing glances from nearby exhibitors. "Bentley has developed seizures. My veterinarian confirmed they're directly related to the hydrocephalus."

Mrs. Blankenship finally deigned to meet Trudy's gaze, her brushing hand suspended mid-stroke. "So you're taking the word of a *veterinarian*"—she spat the word like it tasted foul—"over someone with thirty years of specialized breeding experience?"

My blood pressure spiked. The dismissal of veterinary expertise struck a nerve I hadn't expected.

Trudy faltered momentarily, backing up a step. "Well . . . yes. Bentley's blood work came back normal. The vet says he's too young for epilepsy. Those seizures are directly related to his congenital defect."

"Poppycock! What does *he* know? None of my dogs have ever had seizures. You can't possibly blame this on me or my breeding program."

"But—"

"All dogs have issues, Trudy. There are no guarantees in life." Mrs. Blankenship resumed her brushing, signaling the conversation was beneath her concern.

"But you told me Bentley was perfect. You said he was a top-quality pup. And now you're acting like these seizures are no big deal. He can't be bred, and I'll never recoup the money I spent on him." The anger in Trudy's voice cracked with frustration. "And now I have to give him phenobarbital to control the seizures."

Mrs. Blankenship gave Trudy the same dismissive wave she'd given me earlier. "Nothing's stopping you from breeding him."

Trudy's mouth dropped open, shock replacing frustration. "You *know* that breeding a dog with known seizures would be unethical, Mildred." Her voice hardened. "And *I*, unlike *some* people I know, have ethics! I'm going to report you to the kennel club."

Mrs. Blankenship's jaw tightened. "Be careful what you say, Trudy. I'd hate to have to sue you for slander."

What was it with this woman threatening everyone with lawsuits? Did she have an attorney on speed dial?

"We'll just see about that." Trudy stepped back, trembling with fury. "One day, you'll get yours, Mildred." She turned abruptly, saw me watching the exchange, and shoved past me, muttering, "Mark my words. One day."

Chapter Two

I hustled away before Mrs. Blankenship could spot me, my mind replaying the heated exchange. As much as I hated to admit it, Trudy couldn't definitely prove that Bentley's seizures resulted from his congenital deformity. Many dogs with hydrocephalus lived perfectly normal lives—probably skipping through doggy dreams without a care in the world. I would bet my meager savings that Evangelina Rose had the same condition. Still, a reputable breeder wouldn't outright dismiss a buyer's concerns so callously. If I were in Mrs. Blankenship's designer shoes, I would offer to pay for a full workup by a neurology specialist. Sure, it would cost some money, but it would be worth it in the interest of maintaining good relations and a good name.

I rounded a corner and nearly collided with a parade of golden fur. A group of Golden retrievers competed in the next ring, and I stopped to watch, grateful for the delightful distraction after that toxic interchange I'd just witnessed. Goldens are walking antidepressants—instant mood elevators with tails. I can count on one hand—one finger, actually—the number of Goldens who ever tried to bite me. And I think that dog truly had a neurological malfunction, even though he didn't have seizures. He just had the canine equivalent of waking up on the wrong side of the bed every day of his life.

The dogs in the ring stood proud and ready to please with that unmistakable Golden smile as the judge meticulously examined each one. One dog kept trying to make friends with the judge, much to the dismay of its owner. The judge maintained his professional composure despite being the target of what could only be described as shameless canine flirtation.

"Focus, Buttercup!" hissed the handler of the social butterfly, yanking the leash just enough to redirect the dog's attention. Buttercup responded by sitting perfectly—for about three seconds—before attempting to give the judge's hand a congratulatory lick for his excellent job of . . . well, just existing.

I chuckled. In my book, a dog with that much personality deserved a crown, not just a ribbon. Championship material? According to the rulebook, probably not. Champion of my heart? Absolutely.

I would never fit into the dog show world, where the difference between glory and disappointment hinged on ear-set angles and tail carriage. Yes, I could handle a laceration or a sudden case of gastric distress with veterinary precision, but ask me what qualities made one nearly identical Golden better than another? I'd have better luck explaining quantum physics to a cat. I wondered how Dr. Collins navigated these waters so effortlessly. Perhaps he was a veterinary amphibian, equally comfortable in the clinical and show-ring ponds. Some vets did indeed breed and show dogs, straddling both worlds like furry diplomats.

But to me, all this cut-throat competition seemed to squeeze the joy out of dog ownership faster than stepping on a squeaky toy in my bare feet at 2 AM. Still, I wasn't naive enough to think warm, fuzzy feelings trumped cold, hard cash. A champion show dog could fund a very nice retirement plan.

I couldn't help but wonder what these pedigree enthusiasts would think of my own dog, Sierra—a roadside special whose DNA test would probably come back reading "dog." Found huddled against a guardrail two years ago, she represented exactly zero recognized breeds and approximately infinite amounts of personality. I wouldn't trade her for Westminster's finest, though watching her scratch her ear with her back foot wouldn't exactly impress the judges here.

The Golden retriever judge finally awarded ribbons to three dogs who, to my untrained eye, could have been photocopies of each other. The procession exited the ring with winners lavishing praise on their champions while the ribbon-less handlers displayed emotions ranging from philosophical shoulder shrugs to faces that could curdle milk.

My ears perked up like a German shepherd's when my name crackled over the intercom, summoning me back to the veterinary area. I zigzagged through the crowd, accidentally knocking over someone's popcorn box, creating a feeding frenzy among nearby dogs. Rushing past Mildred Blankenship's grooming table, I caught her mid-sentence: "Hmph. I wouldn't trust my dog to that little snip. She doesn't know what she's doing."

I stopped for a fraction of a second and locked eyes with the woman. Her chin shot upward with the same defiance as a cat who's just knocked your favorite mug off the counter.

She's not worth it. I didn't have time to stand here and try to convince this woman that my veterinary degree wasn't printed on the back of a cereal box. Besides, arguing with Mrs. Blankenship would be like trying to baptize a cat—painful, pointless, and likely to end with someone bleeding.

Biting my lip, I spun on my heel and power-walked to the veterinary station, where a pleasant-looking middle-aged man waited with a handsome Border collie.

"Hello, I'm Dr. Dixon." I extended my hand, and the gentleman shook it. "What can I do for you?"

"Max here had a little mishap in the agility ring," the man explained, nodding toward his Border collie, who sat at perfect attention, looking more dignified than most humans I knew. "Caught his back right leg on one of the jumps."

I knelt to the dog's level, receiving an inspecting sniff followed by reluctant approval. "Sorry to hear that, buddy. Showing off for the ladies in the audience, were you?"

The Border collie cocked his head as if considering whether my joke deserved acknowledgment.

"He was actually leading the competition," the man said, pride evident in his voice. "Sailed through the weave poles like he was made of liquid, then caught his foot on the final jump bar. Tumbled like an Olympic gymnast who'd suddenly remembered a fear of heights."

As I ran my hands over Max's leg, the dog maintained his stoic expression, watching me with eyes that seemed to communicate *I've calculated seventeen escape routes from this room, but I'll humor you for now.* He didn't flinch when I manipulated his limb from paw to hip, but that meant little—some Border collies are so intelligent and focused that an injury would not distract them in the least.

"Would you mind walking him a few steps?" I asked, straightening up with an audible knee crack. "I need to see his gait."

"Certainly. Max, heel." The command was barely necessary. Max moved in perfect synchronization with his owner, matching his stride with military precision. Only when they slowed to a walk did I catch the subtle hitch.

"Let's get him up on the exam table," I said, patting the stainless-steel surface. "Left side down, please."

The man hoisted Max onto the table, and the Border collie dramatically sighed as he was laid on his side, throwing me a look that clearly said, *This indignity will be noted in my memoirs.*

I performed a more thorough examination, my fingers probing through the dense black and white fur while Max endured my touch with the patience of a Buddhist monk.

"There doesn't appear to be anything serious here," I finally announced, straightening up while Max watched me with those unnerving, intelligent eyes. "No fractures, dislocations, or ligament tears." I scratched behind his ears, earning a reluctant thump of his tail.

"So, he'll be okay?" Relief flooded the man's face.

"Just a soft tissue injury—the canine equivalent of a pulled muscle. I can give him an anti-inflammatory medication you can give as needed."

The man lifted Max down, and the Border collie immediately resumed his dignified sitting position, though I caught him testing his weight on the injured leg when he thought no one was looking. Classic Border collie. He'd rather gnaw off his own leg than admit weakness.

"What do I owe you?" The man reached for his wallet, unleashing a cascade of business cards that fluttered to the floor like rectangular snowflakes.

I waved him off while helping collect the scattered cards. "The show covers my services." At least I hoped so—I'd neglected to clarify that minor detail with Dr. Collins' wife.

The man nodded gratefully, then plucked a card from the pile and handed it to me. "I appreciate your help. If I can ever return the favor, don't hesitate to call."

I glanced at the card, then did a double-take. Cliff Granger, Criminal Defense Attorney. The card was heavy cardstock with raised lettering—the kind that cost more than my monthly coffee budget.

"Well, thank you, Mr. Granger," I said with a laugh, tucking the card into my pocket. "But I'm hoping to keep my criminal career limited to stealing extra packets of ketchup from fast food restaurants. I don't expect to need your services."

He smiled—not the shark-like grin I'd expected from a criminal defense attorney, but something warm and genuine that transformed his conventional features. With his cable-knit sweater and sensible shoes, he looked more like a high school math teacher than someone who defended potential murderers.

"Keep it," he said with a meaningful nod. "You never know."

I stared after him as he and Max walked away, the Border collie's limp mysteriously vanished. *You never know?* What exactly did *that* mean? Was he predicting my imminent descent into a life of crime?

I shook my head. Just what I needed—cryptic warnings from a man who defended people who probably had bodies buried in their backyards.

My thoughts were interrupted by a large man wearing an ill-fitting suit charging through the crowd.

"Where is she? Where is that witch? I know she's here somewhere!"

Dear Lord, what now? The drama in this place far outshone any daytime soap opera.

Another man interceded him, laying a hand on his arm. "Who are you looking for?"

"Mildred Blankenship, that's who!"

Oh. My. Goodness. Another Battleship fan.

"She's set up down there." Another man helpfully ratted her out with a pointed finger.

"Wait," said the man who still hung on to the big man's arm. "What are you going to do?"

The big man shook the hand off. "I'm going to get my money, that's what!" He stomped off with fire burning in his eyes.

Yeah, I know I should have minded my own business and stayed out of it. But naturally, I didn't. Curiosity overrode common sense, and I slipped off after him. Nick caught my eye and hustled around the vendor's stand to join me.

"Do you know that guy?" I asked.

Nick nodded. "Martin Billings. He used to be the Battleship's handler."

"So, what happened?" We quickened our steps to keep up with Martin Billings.

"I'm not sure. I just know that this year, she's showing all her dogs herself."

The big man zeroed in on Mrs. Blankenship, who was still obsessively brushing the same dog. Gracious, how much fluff could one tiny dog have?

"Mildred!" he barked.

She looked up, clearly unruffled, as if a raging bull wasn't standing two feet away. "Marty," she greeted coolly. "How nice to see you. I didn't realize we were still on speaking terms. To what do I owe this pleasure?" Although she used the word "pleasure," she made it sound more like an impending root canal performed by an intern on their first day.

Martin's jaw clenched, a muscle in his cheek twitching. "You know why I'm here. You still owe me ten thousand dollars."

I gasped, then clamped my hand over my mouth. *Ten thousand dollars*? What had she done? Sold him a box full of defective puppies?

Her eyes flicked over him, unbothered. "I already told you, Marty, that the dogs weren't performing to standard. You didn't live up to your end of the bargain."

He took a step closer, invading her personal space. "I did my job. I gave your dogs the training they needed, but you still stiffed me. It's been months. How long are you planning to drag this out?"

She shot him a snarky smile. "I don't pay for failures, Marty."

"We made a deal, Mildred."

She waved that dismissive hand again. She certainly was a pro with that hand. That gesture had obviously been developed over a long time. "There's no written contract."

Marty's nostrils flared. "I'm a man of my word. And I expect other people to keep their word."

She swept the Chihuahua off the grooming table and placed it in a crate, turning her back on the man. "I don't have time for this, Marty. My group is up next. And I intend to win that blue ribbon despite your less-than-stellar results."

He leaned in and lowered his voice, making it sound more ominous than when he was shouting. "You think you're above paying your debts?" He took another step forward, blocking her between the grooming table and the crate. "You think you can do whatever you want without consequences?"

Without thinking, I grabbed Nick's arm. Sure, I didn't like the old bat, but I didn't want to see Marty rearrange her facial features right before my eyes. It probably should have occurred to me to go for help, but I was so transfixed by the scene I couldn't move.

I needn't have been concerned. Mildred gave him a hefty shove, and he stumbled backward. "Get out of my way. I'll pay you when I feel like it, although you didn't do anything to earn your fee."

Marty's face twisted with a mixture of frustration and something darker. "Oh, you'll pay me, Mildred."

She ignored him and plucked another dog from a crate—Evangelina Rose, who didn't appear any worse for wear from her traumatic toenail injury.

"So, sue me. Without anything in writing, it's your word against mine."

Oh. That was a twist. This time, she invited someone to sue *her*. Should I pass along Mr. Granger's card? No, a criminal defense attorney probably wouldn't be interested in a lawsuit over a broken agreement.

She pushed past Mr. Billings, who looked about ready to explode. His hands balled into fists at his sides. "You'll regret this, Mildred."

Chapter Three

Nick turned to return to his vendor's booth, but I held back, inexplicably drawn to what promised to be the canine world's version of a WWE smackdown. For some baffling reason, I wanted to see Mrs. Blankenship and Evangelina Rose compete. Call me a glutton for punishment.

Nick paused. "What?"

"I want to see the Chihuahua competition." Even as the words left my mouth, I questioned my own sanity.

He shook his head with the weary resignation of a man who'd witnessed too many dog show atrocities. "Why?"

I shrugged. "Beats me."

He sighed. "I can tell you who will win. For reasons only God and possibly the devil know, the Battleship will win."

"I don't get it. What does she have on the judges? Compromising photos? Blackmail material?"

"I have no idea. I don't think she's sleeping with them." He grinned at his own joke.

I choked so violently on my saliva that a nearby poodle owner threw me a concerned look. My face flamed. The very image of the formidable woman . . .

"Thanks, Nick. I will never get that picture out of my mind. I may need therapy."

He looked less than chagrinned. "Sorry. Maybe she bribes them. You know, slips them envelopes full of cash behind the porta-potties."

The thought disturbed me greatly, although with refusing refunds on defective puppies and not paying her handler, she probably had cash to spare. "Aren't the judges supposed to be impartial?"

"Supposedly, but who's to say? This is a cutthroat world."

My rose-colored glasses slipped a little. "Well, if that's true, it disappoints me. Some things should be above reproach, like dog shows and the Olympics."

"I didn't say it was true." He ran a hand through his hair, messing it in a way that was oddly appealing. "Look, I'll walk over with you and watch. But I promise you, the Battleship will win. Bookies won't even take bets on this match."

I raised my eyebrows.

"Just kidding. No bookies operate at dog shows— as far as I know."

We made our way to the ring, dodging a Great Pyrenees, which lay in the middle of the aisle, stubbornly refusing to move. Several Chihuahuas paraded with their owners, each of whom was large. I made a mental note to observe the Great Dane competition to see if the owners were petite.

I spotted the woman who had spoken harshly of Mildred Blankenship's wins earlier that morning.

Determination was etched on her face as she marched her tiny dog—presumably Clementine—around the circle, occasionally side-eyeing her competition with malicious looks. I tried to gauge the championship qualities of Evangelina Rose versus Clementine, but couldn't come up with anything objective.

Mrs. Blankenship wore an expression of pure cockiness with an arrogant tilt of her head. She didn't so much walk as strut, her considerable frame sending tremors through the floor that made nearby water bottles quake in response. The judge, a man in a bow tie that seemed to be strangling him, took forever as he thoroughly inspected each dog, squinting through Coke bottle glasses. Finally, he strode to the table and retrieved the ribbons with the gravity of someone announcing the winner at the Academy Awards. As Nick had predicted, the blue ribbon went to Evangelina Rose. Second place went to Clementine, whose owner sagged with disappointment. But only for a moment.

As the contenders filed out of the ring, Clementine's owner reached out and grabbed Mildred Blankenship's arm.

"You're a cheat, Mildred," she spat, her voice laced with venom. "And you know it."

Mildred looked with disdain at the hand clutching her arm and shook it off as if she were discarding a piece of dog fur. "You should really work on that bitterness, Darlene. It's aging you." She tried to move away, but the crowd blocked her, unwilling to miss the drama.

The woman, whom I now knew was named Darlene, pressed in closer, close enough that Evangelina Rose's eyes widened. She ducked her tiny head deeper into its resting place. "You bribed the judge again."

Mrs. Blankenship turned, arching a brow. "And where is your proof? Oh, that's right. You don't have any. Just like you don't have any blue ribbons."

Darlene reached down and scooped up her little dog, who was in danger of being trampled by all the rubberneckers pressing in for a better view. "People talk, Mildred. And when the truth comes out, you'll be the one who loses. Everything."

Mildred smirked, tucking Evangelina Rose deeper in her bosom. "The truth? The truth is, you're a washed-up has-been clinging to dogs who will never be champions. Face it, Darlene. You lost. You always lose."

Darlene's breath came fast and sharp, her face turning the color of a ripe tomato. "If I were you, I'd watch my back."

Mildred's smirk widened, but her eyes remained cold. "Oh, Darlene. I *never* take my eyes off the competition." She huffed out a mirthless laugh that sent a nearby Yorkie diving for cover under a chair. "Not that I'm worried about *you*."

Darlene managed to push her way through the crowd with the determination of a subway commuter at rush hour, nearly knocking over a man carrying several cups of coffee in a precarious stack.

Mildred stroked the domed head between her breasts. "Good girl, Evangelina Rose. We did it again."

"My goodness," I whispered to Nick as we backed away from the scene. "The woman seems to deliberately do everything under the sun to provoke people. I'm glad it's not just me she dislikes."

He laughed. "Don't take it personally. You're in good company. Mother Teresa and the Pope are probably on her list, too."

I shook my head. "I should probably get back to my station."

He glanced at his watch. "Yikes! It's almost lunchtime. I've probably got a line at the hot dog stand." He took off without waiting for me, then called over his shoulder, "After the rush, I'll bring you a hot dog."

I grinned. The way he said it made it sound like a gourmet meal instead of meat of questionable origin in a bun that had been sitting under a heat lamp for who knows how long.

When I returned to the veterinary area, I found a distraught young woman pacing back and forth, a blond Cocker spaniel matching her steps.

"I'm sorry," I said, sliding behind my exam table. "Were you waiting for me?"

Her head popped up. "Oh, yes. Are you the vet? Please tell me you're the vet and not just someone who wandered in here looking for the restroom."

"Yes. Dr. Amy Dixon." I stuck out my hand, but she had already turned aside to fish something from a huge tote bag on her shoulder.

She finally extracted a medicine vial and held it out to me, her hand trembling slightly. "I don't know how I could have been so careless. I guess with the excitement of coming all this way to the dog show, I simply forgot to have this refilled. I remembered my curling iron, Simon's dog shampoo, and all my shoes, but not Simon's medication."

I took the vial and read the label. Phenobarbital. As

empty as my bank account. I frowned. "I didn't think you could show dogs who have seizures."

"Well, technically, it depends on the judge and what is causing the seizures. But Simon is competing in agility. And he's neutered." She riffled again through the bag and produced a health certificate from her veterinarian. "I'm worried that the stress of being here will trigger his seizures."

"When's the last time he had his pill?" I asked, while Simon gave me a look that seemed to say, *Please, lady, can you give* her *a sedative, too?*

"This morning. But I don't have any left."

"I can give you enough pills to get you through. When will you be home?"

The tension left her body so quickly that I was afraid she'd collapse. "Oh, thank you. You're a lifesaver. I'll be home on Sunday."

"However, I do need to do an exam on Simon before I can prescribe medication. Can you put him on the table?"

"Yes, of course." She lifted Simon, who gave me a resigned look that said, *Please, no thermometer.*

"So," I said, beginning my examination, "what's your name, and how long has Simon had seizures?" I ran my hands gently over his body.

"I'm Kaitlyn Tanner. Simon started having them about a year ago. My vet back home said it's idiopathic epilepsy." She stroked Simon's head. "The first time he had one, I got so scared I called 911 and tried to do CPR before I realized it wasn't helping." She gave a nervous laugh. "The dispatcher was very understanding. She's a dog owner, too."

Simon, meanwhile, seemed to enjoy being in the

hands of someone not hysterical, as his nubby little tail wagged with enthusiasm.

"Well, he looks healthy," I said, peeking into his ears, which were surprisingly clean for a Cocker spaniel. Simon had to be the one in a hundred Cocker spaniels without an ear infection. "And his teeth look great. You must brush them."

"Thank you. I do."

I pulled my stethoscope from around my neck and listened to Simon's heart, hearing a good and steady lub-dub, lub-dub.

Replacing my stethoscope around my neck, I said, "You can take him down." I dug through my purse for the key to the controlled drug box. After opening it, I pulled out the half-grain phenobarbital bottle, twisted off the cap, and counted out ten pills—enough to get Simon through the next few days until Kaitlyn could get a refill.

Just as I dropped the pills into Kaitlyn's empty vial, a page came over the speaker. "Dr. Dixon to the agility area, STAT!"

Chapter Four

Oh dear! **My** heart started racing as I thrust the pill bottle into Kaitlyn's hand and grabbed my medical bag. I took off toward the other end of the building where the agility trials were being held, weaving through throngs of people and trying not to trip on leashes.

A tight knot of people huddled in the center of the agility field. A vet can always tell where the action is by the number of people gathered around the scene.

I parted the group like Moses parting the Red Sea, saying, "Excuse me, let me through, please," until I came upon the emergency.

A beautiful, white standard poodle lay in a widening puddle of blood. "What happened?" I dropped to my knees, yanking gloves onto my hands.

"Fiona caught her leg on something sharp," said a young woman with tears running down her cheeks.

"Are you the owner?" I grabbed a towel and pressed it against the wound, but crimson soaked through instantly. White fur, drenched and clumped, made it impossible to see the source of the bleeding. I swept my fingers through the wet mess until something caught my eye. There. A severed blood vessel spurted red from somewhere below the stifle.

"Yes, I'm Candace Bates."

"I'm Dr. Amy Dixon. I'll need to sedate Fiona and tie off that bleeding blood vessel," I said, reaching for a tourniquet and applying it proximal to the bleeder. "Can someone carry her to the veterinary station?"

"I will." A young man stepped forward, and his face went deathly pale. Then his knees buckled, and he sank to the floor, his head missing the edge of the ramp by mere inches.

Great. Now I had *two* emergencies. And I didn't do people medicine. People were gross.

"Someone get a cold, wet cloth for that man," I ordered. "And I need another volunteer to carry Fiona."

Another man hefted Fiona into his arms. Candace and I trotted after him to the vet station.

"Will Fiona be all right? She's lost so much blood." The worried owner choked on a sob.

"She should be fine," I said. "It looks worse than it is. Blood just shows up more on white dogs." Now, I hoped I was right.

We reached the veterinary aid station, and I directed the man to lay Fiona on the table. The onlookers gathered like vultures to roadkill. Thank heavens for the privacy curtain, which I yanked closed with enough force to nearly pull the rings off the rod.

"Show's over, folks," I muttered under my breath. "No tickets available."

I should have cut them some slack. I did the same thing when I slowed to gawk at a car accident. But that was just to assure myself that everyone was okay. Or so I told myself.

I grabbed for my controlled drug box, momentarily dismayed when I saw the lid open and the key still dangling in the lock. *Smooth move, Dr. Dixon. Just broadcast to the world you've got the good stuff.* In the chaos of the emergency call, I'd committed the cardinal sin of veterinary medicine. I mentally filed that blunder away under "things my professor would slap me for" and quickly assessed Fiona's weight.

"Had Fiona eaten today?" I asked Candace, trying to maintain a modicum of professionalism.

She shook her head. "No. I didn't want her doing agility with a full stomach."

"Good. We shouldn't have to worry about her vomiting." I drew up a dose of Dexdomitor with Torgesic and gave the injection in Fiona's thigh muscle. "This is a reversible sedative with additional pain medication. She'll be floating on cloud nine in about five minutes."

I looked up as the curtain parted, and a middle-aged woman approached. "I'm a vet tech. Do you need some help?"

I raised my eyes upward. *Thank You, God.* Relief swept over me. I could handle this injury solo, sure, but not having to do surgery and monitor anesthesia at the same time made my job a lot easier. I welcomed another pair of professional hands.

"Yes, thank you. She has a torn artery that needs to be tied off. I've just given her Dexdomitor and Torgesic."

The woman nodded. "I'm Debbie." She extended her hand before apparently eyeballing my bloody gloves and thinking better of it. "Where are the gloves and the clippers?"

I directed her to the supply box and handed over my stethoscope. Turning to Candace, who looked like she might faint, puke, or both, I said, "Do you want to stay and watch, or would you be more comfortable waiting outside?" Like I said, I didn't treat humans.

Her eyes darted back and forth between me and the dog. "I'll stay if it's okay."

I suddenly remembered the Good Samaritan who'd carried Fiona in. He stood awkwardly to the side, his shirt and arms looking like he'd walked straight off the set of a slasher film. "Oh, sir, thank you so much for your help. We're fine if you want to go hose yourself off."

"Yeah." He grimaced, examining his saturated shirt. "I just might do that. I look like I've been in a massacre."

It was then that I realized I hadn't gotten Candace to sign for permission for sedation and treatment. Another cardinal sin. What was the matter with me? Was I trying for the most negligent vet award?

As Fiona's head began to droop and her eyes glazed over in narcotic bliss, I whipped out a permission form and a pen, shoving it into Candace's hand. "I need you to sign the consent form for sedation and treatment."

If she thought it odd that I produced the form *after* I'd already sedated Fiona, mercifully, she kept it to herself. She scribbled her signature and gave the paper back to me.

Fiona's body completely relaxed, and Debbie laid a towel across her eyes. Sometimes, dogs under Dexdomitor could be startled by sounds and lights, so the towel helped block out sensory stimuli. She checked

Fiona's gum color, heartbeat, and respirations before reaching for the clippers to shave the wound area.

Leaving the prep in her capable hands, I opened a surgical pack, drape, and suture packs, and pulled on fresh gloves. Once the bloody, matted hair was clipped away, I could finally see what I was dealing with. Debbie quickly scrubbed and rinsed the surrounding tissue, then I laid the sterile drape over the surgical field.

"Okay. Let's find this pesky bleeder. Debbie, would you release the tourniquet slowly?" Debbie complied, and the wicked little blood vessel squirted me in the eye like a water gun.

"Argh!" I sputtered as Debbie retightened the tourniquet.

I wiped my face with my sleeve. "Let's try that again. I think my GPS has narrowed in on that artery now."

Round two. Debbie loosened the tourniquet, and once again, the vessel showered me in the face before I successfully clamped it off.

"Got ya!" I opened a suture pack and triumphantly placed a ligature around the troublesome vessel, then released the clamp. Yay! No more blood fountain.

Debbie removed the tourniquet and moved to Fiona's head. "Color's good. Pulse is 50, respirations 12."

I nodded. Dexdomitor could greatly decrease pulse and respiration, but those rates were perfectly acceptable. I sutured the rest of the wound, which had clean edges, indicating something sharp had caused the damage.

"All done," I announced, snapping off my gloves

with a dramatic snap. Debbie immediately began cleaning the rest of the blood off Fiona, who now resembled less of a horror movie prop.

I turned to Candace and said, "Everything looks good. I'll bandage her leg and wake her up. She should be on her feet in a few minutes. But I'm afraid her Olympic dreams are dashed for today."

"That's for sure," said Candace. "We're going straight home. And possibly into retirement from dog shows."

I drew up a dose of Antisedan to reverse the effects of the sedative and injected it into Fiona's thigh before applying a pressure bandage to her leg.

"Try to leave the bandage on until tomorrow. Then it can come off. The stitches will need to come out in seven to ten days at your regular vet's office. I'll send you home with a few days' worth of antibiotics and pain medication. Is there anything Fiona can't take?"

"No, she's always been healthy."

Debbie gently transferred Fiona to the floor, and Candace immediately assumed the position of a cross-legged guardian angel, stroking Fiona's back. I was glad she hadn't passed out or thrown up.

"Is there anything else I can do for you, Doc?"

"No, thank you so much, Debbie. You certainly came along at the right time."

"In that case, I'm going to go back to the agility area and see if I can find what Fiona injured herself on."

"Good idea. We don't need any repeats of this episode."

Debbie took her leave, and I cleaned up the surgical area while waiting for Fiona to wake up. The open controlled drug box caught my eye, and I stopped what I was doing to log in the medications I had used and dispensed before locking it and securing the key back in my purse.

The thumping of a tail against concrete alerted me to Fiona's return to the conscious world. The tail was often the first thing to "wake up" under Dexdomitor. I crouched beside the limp dog and whispered, "Earth to Fiona, come in, Fiona." Her ears twitched, and her eyes fluttered open with the confusion of someone waking up in a strange motel room. She attempted to lift her head but was still wobbly.

"She'll be up shortly."

Candace smiled for the first time since the accident. "Thank you so much for saving her life. I was so scared."

I squeezed her shoulder. "You're quite welcome. Fiona may be a little groggy for a few hours, so no food or water until she's fully with us."

"I'm just grateful you were here."

"It's my job. That's why I get paid the big . . . so-so bucks." Even if I *couldn't* fix a broken toenail on Evangelina Rose, I had managed to keep Fiona from bleeding out on the agility course.

Fiona rolled to her chest, then struggled to get her feet under her. She rose on trembling legs, like a newborn colt, then gave a full body shake as she gazed at her owner with a *What happened?* look. She took a few unsteady steps, then raised her rear leg sporting the bandage, staring at it in bewilderment.

I laughed. "You're okay, Fiona. Your leg is still attached and functional. No need to give it the stink eye." She shook the leg, then set it down gingerly.

"You can take her home now."

Candace gripped my hands. "Thank you again, Dr. Dixon." She snapped Fiona's leash to her harness and led her out, with Fiona goose-stepping on her bandaged leg.

I pulled back the curtain and finished cleaning up. A few minutes later, Nick appeared carrying two hot dogs, a soda, and a chocolate bar.

"Talk about a lifesaver," I said, suddenly realizing I was hungry enough to eat the paper wrappers, too. "This is just what the doctor ordered." I started to take a big bite of the hot dog.

He stopped and stared at my face. "Whoa! How's the other guy look?"

I paused mid-bite. "What?"

"You might want to check a mirror."

My eyes narrowed as I set my hot dog on the table and rummaged in my purse for my makeup mirror. Holy smokes! I looked like I'd gone a round or two with Muhammad Ali. Blood spatter decorated my face like abstract art, with particular emphasis on my forehead and chin.

"Cripes! Why didn't anyone tell me?" I frantically grabbed a hand wipe and began to work on the damage.

"I just did," Nick said, helping himself to a bite of my abandoned hot dog. "Good thing, too, before you walked around looking like Carrie at the prom."

I cringed, imagining people's reaction if they saw me like this. Particularly the Battleship. Though why I was obsessing over the opinion of a woman who clearly thought I was one lab coat short of a veterinary degree, I couldn't say.

"Give me that." I snatched my hot dog out of

Nick's hand. "Blood spattered or not, a doctor needs to keep up her energy."

Chapter Five

I gobbled down my hot dog with less-than-ladylike manners, ketchup dotting the corner of my mouth and mustard somehow finding its way onto my sleeve. If Nick thought less of me, he was polite enough not to comment. I filled him in on Fiona's injury.

"Sounds like you saved the day," he said, his eyes twinkling in admiration.

As much as I wanted him to view me as a superhero, the surgery wasn't all that spectacular in the big scheme of things. "Not really. It looked a lot worse than it actually was."

"Still, I bet Fiona's owner thought otherwise."

Candace *had* been grateful, and that warm, fuzzy feeling of helping someone in need still lingered. "I hope the rest of the day is uneventful."

He chuckled. "Oh, there's always something going on to create drama. Dog shows are like soap operas with better hair—and I'm talking about the dogs."

As if on cue, a red-faced woman wearing a paisley dress two sizes too small stomped by us, her chunky heels echoing off the concrete. "I'm going to *kill* her!" she muttered with venomous intensity.

Nick raised his eyebrows. "See, what did I tell

you?"

We exchanged a look that perfectly communicated mutual curiosity and mild concern for public safety. Without a word, we abandoned our food wrappers and power-walked on the heels of the irate woman, staying just far enough back to avoid being swept into her vortex of rage. Not surprisingly, her warpath led directly to Mrs. Blankenship, who sat picking at a salad.

"Mildred! I need to speak to you!" The woman's voice carried with such force that three nearby Yorkshire Terriers simultaneously cowered under their grooming tables.

Mrs. Blankenship's lips puckered like she'd bitten into a sour pickle, and she set down her fork. "Joanna. How lovely to see you." Her expression said otherwise. "I didn't know you were showing today."

Joanna's eyes blazed with fury. "I'm not. I came to deliver a puppy to Randy Parks. But when I got here, he said he changed his mind and wanted his deposit back. Funny how that happened right after you had lunch with him yesterday."

"I'm sorry to hear that." Mildred's sympathy had all the warmth of an iceberg in January.

"Cut the act, Mildred." Joanna slammed her purse onto the table, sending Mildred's coffee thermos wobbling dangerously.

Mildred glared at the thermos, and it stopped moving like one of her misbehaving dogs.

"It's because of the lies you've been spreading about me. About my dogs. About my breeding program."

Mrs. Blankenship raised a brow. "Lies? My dear Joanna, I've never spoken anything but the truth. Not everyone appreciates . . . enthusiastic breeding techniques." She emphasized the word "enthusiastic" like it was code for "puppy mill."

Joanna's fists clenched at her sides. "You've been telling people that my dogs are overbred. That my dogs are genetically flawed. That my bloodlines are unstable." The woman's voice wobbled with rage, her face flushing crimson. "You called me an *amateur*—to the president of the regional kennel club, no less."

Mildred offered an icy smile, her eyes unblinking. "I was merely offering some constructive criticism."

"To everyone *but* me." Joanna's nostrils flared like an angry bull.

I instinctively took a step back, pulling Nick with me.

Joanna went on. "You know as well as I do that I've been in this business longer than you have. I showed you the ropes, for crying out loud. I was breeding champions when you were still begging judges for participation ribbons!"

"Yet your dogs aren't nearly as refined as mine." Mildred examined her manicure. "You're too attached to your emotions, Joanna. The ring doesn't lie."

Joanna took a step closer, but Mildred held her ground like a marble statue. "You've been doing this for years. You've sabotaged my reputation every chance you got. But this time, it's gone too far."

Mildred crossed her arms, her face a perfect mask of indifference. "As the saying goes, Joanna, 'if you can't stand the heat, stop letting your dogs inbreed.'"

I choked on air, trying to muffle the sound of my coughs. Nick discreetly thumped me on the back.

Joanna's voice dropped low and intimidating.

"You think you can ruin me, Mildred?"

"Oh, Joanna." Mildred sighed dramatically as if dealing with a slow child. "You're ruining yourself. All by yourself."

Joanna stepped back, her face contorting with renewed fury. Her eyes fixed on Mildred like a predator eyeing prey. "Just know, I'm not going anywhere. And I'm going to make sure the truth about you comes out."

Mildred tilted her head. "Is that a threat, Joanna? Because if you think for one minute that I'm afraid of you—"

"You *should* be afraid, Mildred. Because I'm going to ensure you don't get away with your vicious slander anymore."

The dismissive hand that I had come to know so well in such a short time shot up like a crossing guard stopping traffic. "We'll see about that, won't we?"

Joanna's jaw tightened, but apparently, she could find nothing more to say as she quickly spun on her heel and stalked off, leaving Nick and me exposed as eavesdroppers. Uh-oh. I felt like a deer caught in the headlights of Mildred's laser glare.

Her eyes zeroed in on us. "What are *you* looking at?"

I feigned innocence. "Nothing. We were simply walking by on our way to see the Doberman competition. Right, Nick?" I elbowed him harder than necessary.

"Oh. Yes. Dobermans," Nick stammered unconvincingly. "I love Dobermans."

Her lips curled in a sneer. "The Doberman competition is *that* way." She gestured with her chin to the opposite end of the fairgrounds.

"Oh. Thank you." I grabbed Nick's arm. "We're in the wrong place, Nick. Hurry. We don't want to miss the Dobermans." I started to drag him away.

"You already did," she said. "It was this morning. Next time, try reading the program instead of eavesdropping on private conversations."

Private conversation? The exchange was loud enough to be heard in the parking lot.

My face heated, but I forced myself to continue the charade. "Oh, shoot. Well, let's see what else is going on." I yanked Nick's arm, eager to be as far away from the woman as possible.

We'd gotten out of Mrs. Blankenship's line of sight when Nick burst out laughing.

"It's not funny," I hissed, slapping his shoulder. "She already hates me, and now she knows I was listening in." I belatedly realized I probably shouldn't have slapped his shoulder. I'd only just met the man that morning, and although his good looks made my insides flutter, my action could have been perceived as flirtatious. Or hostile. This whole day had me completely discombobulated, and I longed to get back to my normal routine.

But he continued to chuckle. "So what? She wouldn't like you better if you hadn't listened in."

He had a point. Besides, with any luck and a merciful Heavenly Father, I would never have to see the woman again after today. Though knowing my luck, she'd show up as my new next-door neighbor.

A Scripture verse sprang to mind about loving one's enemies and praying for those who persecuted you. Would it be wrong to pray that I never had to see Mrs. Blankenship again? As for loving her, well, after seeing all the people who wished her ill will, I needed to reach deep into my heart and find some modicum of kindness for the woman. But it was a mighty long reach.

I grabbed Nick's arm again. "Come on. After that encounter, I'm in desperate need of ice cream. I sure hope the snack bar has some." My fingers lingered on his forearm a few seconds too long. Honestly, I needed to stop touching this man.

He grinned. "It does, indeed. Your wish is my command."

"I'll buy," I said, trying not to come across as pushy and presumptuous. But he *had* brought me a hot dog, after all. Didn't that action say something about his interest in me? I wanted to think so. But I didn't want him to think I was only interested in him for what he could give me—free concession stand food.

"Not necessary." He led me behind the snack bar counter and flipped open the freezer lid. A blast of frosty air hit my face as he gestured to a frozen treasure trove of ice cream sandwiches, popsicles, and drumsticks. "Take your pick."

I selected a drumstick, peeled back the wrapper, and took a bite. "Mmm. Ice cream fixes almost anything."

"Agreed." He started to unwrap an ice cream sandwich when two giggling teenage girls approached the snack bar, their eyelashes fluttering with such vigor they could have generated electricity. They requested popcorn while practically hanging over the counter. It seemed to me they wanted the attention of the popcorn seller more than the popcorn, but then who was I to judge?

"I'll let you get back to work," I said, backing away from the snack bar, holding my drumstick aloft.

"See you later?" he called over the heads of his admirers.

Warmth flooded through my insides, and I smiled. "Sure." Yep, from the malevolent stares coming my way from the teenage girls, they definitely had more than popcorn on the brain.

I sank into my chair behind the portable exam table and devoured my drumstick, feeling much better after another run-in with Mrs. Battleship. Glancing at my watch, I was relieved to see that I only had three more hours to go. Hopefully, Fiona would be my biggest excitement for the day, and I could go home and take a nice, long bath—but not before slipping Nick my business card with my personal cell number inked on the back.

Nick stayed busy with customers the rest of the afternoon, so I divided my time between wandering back and forth to the opposite end of the fairgrounds from Mrs. Blankenship and returning text messages. After today, I couldn't wait to leave the dog-eat-dog competition world and get back to treating flea allergies and ear infections. I did have some dog breeder clients, but they were nothing like some of the people I'd seen today.

At five-fifty-five, I started to pack up my supplies with the speed of someone fleeing a crime scene. Then, Mr. Wigglesworth came barreling toward me like his pants were on fire, arms waving wildly.

"We need you right away," he gasped, nearly colliding with the table. "There's something wrong with Mrs. Blankenship."

I recoiled. "Wh . . . what do you mean?" Had she tripped over her own tongue?

He clutched at my sleeve. "She's collapsed in her chair. Come *on!*" He tugged with surprising strength for a man named Wigglesworth.

I dug in my heels like a stubborn mule. "But I'm a *vet,* not a physician. Did you call 911?" My voice rose to a pitch only dogs could hear.

"Yes, of course we did. But until they send someone, you're the only medical professional around." We engaged in a back-and-forth tug of war as he tried to move me forward and I tried to grow roots into the concrete.

Now, I will admit that despite the fact I'm not a people doctor, that hasn't stopped people from seeking my advice from time to time, and mostly, my advice consisted of telling them to consult a physician. And, yes, I knew basic first aid, which amounted mostly to applying Band-Aids and putting ice on injuries. But I *couldn't,* I just *couldn't* be expected to try to render medical assistance to a woman who wouldn't let me near her *dog.* If she saw me, her blood pressure would probably go through the roof, and she'd have a stroke, which would be all my fault. Then I'd be known forever as "that vet who killed Mrs. Blankenship."

"I didn't hear a page for a doctor or nurse," I argued as Mr. Wigglesworth managed to dislodge me from my foothold with a yank that nearly dislocated my shoulder, and I found myself being dragged toward the Battleship.

Just then, the PA system crackled. "Is there a doctor in the house? We need a doctor at the north end of the fairgrounds, STAT."

Good. Surely, with this many people, there had to be a doctor or nurse among them. Even a dentist or a chiropractor would do. I'd even take a first-year medical student. But as we moved quickly toward Mrs. Blankenship, I noted, with a sinking heart, that the crowd had thinned out considerably as the day's events had concluded. In fact, very few people remained. My own pulse skyrocketed, and my stomach threatened to give up my earlier indulgences of junk food.

We reached the area where the Battleship had been anchored for most of the day. The woman lay slumped back in her camp chair, her head lolling unnaturally to one side like a broken bobblehead. Her arms hung limply at her sides. An overturned coffee thermos lay on the floor, a dark stain spreading across the concrete.

"Mrs. Blankenship!" I gave her shoulder a firm shake, half expecting her to spring up and accuse me of assault. "Mrs. Blankenship, can you hear me?" *Please, dear God, send a doctor. I can't do this.*

"Do you think she had a heart attack?" asked Mr. Wigglesworth, hopping from one foot to the other as if he needed a restroom.

"I don't know." With a trembling hand that mimicked a caffeine overdose, I reached out and laid my fingers against her neck. Her skin felt cold, but I forced myself to search for a pulse despite my rising panic. I didn't feel anything, but I couldn't be sure if it was because of my shaking hand, very low blood pressure, or worse. Turning my head, I tried to assess whether or not she was breathing. Not seeing her chest rise or fall, I pulled my stethoscope from around my neck and placed it against her chest, painfully aware of my intrusiveness. Where did one auscultate people's hearts, anyway? I moved the diaphragm of my stethoscope over several different sites but heard nothing but the terrified beat of my own heart.

"Help me get her onto the floor," I yelled to several frozen bystanders who stood gaping like visitors at a zoo. A couple of men came forward and took the woman's arms, lowering her onto her back on the concrete as I cradled her head. Then they stepped back faster than if she'd burst into flames.

Putting aside my distaste, I straddled Mrs. Blankenship's unresponsive body and began performing CPR, silently apologizing with every downward thrust. I didn't know whether to pray I could revive her—in which case she would most assuredly sue me for molesting her—or pray I couldn't. Still, I had to try. Despite my dislike for the woman, she deserved a chance. I brought my mouth to hers and breathed into it, trying not to gag with revulsion. Then I resumed chest compressions. Although a small crowd had gathered to watch the performance, no one offered to help.

It seemed like an eternity—or several eternities stacked on top of each other—before the paramedics arrived. By then, sweat poured down my face, my hair looked like I'd stuck my finger in a light socket, and my arms felt like overcooked spaghetti. Gratefully, I relinquished the job to the paramedics as I collapsed, drained on the cold floor. They hefted her onto a gurney and wheeled her away with impressive speed, with one man continuing CPR.

The show over, the small crowd began to disperse. Somewhat disoriented and dizzy as my adrenaline dropped like a skydiver without a parachute, I caught snatches of conversation.

"Well, the old crone finally got what was coming to her."

"I doubt it was a heart attack. She didn't have a heart."

"I'll bet there'll be precious few mourners at her funeral. Probably just her dogs, and they'll have to be bribed with treats."

"Good riddance. Now, maybe someone deserving can win the best in show."

Wow. I had little love for the woman, but I never wished her dead. I couldn't believe the insensitivity of those who had just witnessed the death of a human being. Apparently, Mrs. Blankenship had made a lot of enemies over the years. As I sat there catching my breath, I couldn't help but wonder if being Top Dog in the dog show world was really worth dying alone on a concrete floor, mourned by no one but a reluctant veterinarian with spaghetti arms.

Chapter Six

Nick found me still sitting in the same place several minutes later, staring blankly at nothing in particular.

"What happened?" he asked, slightly out of breath. "I was loading up my van, and suddenly I saw the paramedics wheeling out Mrs. Blankenship doing CPR."

"I don't know for sure," I said, my voice flat, like all the emotion had been wrung out of it. "Mr. Wigglesworth came and got me—told me something was wrong with her. When I got to her, she was unresponsive, and I couldn't find a heartbeat. I did CPR until I thought my arms would fall off."

He sank next to me with a grunt. "Wow. Everyone thought she was too mean to die."

I shot him a glare.

He held his hands up in surrender. "Sorry, that remark was uncalled for and inappropriate, especially given the circumstances. Plus, we don't even know for sure she's gone."

"It didn't look good," I said.

Suddenly, in the ensuing quiet, I heard a whimpering noise.

We both turned. There, pressed between a crate and the wall, sat Evangelina Rose. She regarded us with large eyes and wide pupils, her large ears flat against her head like she was trying to disappear into the concrete.

"Oh, sweetie . . ." I rose and slowly approached the confused animal, crouching as I went. "It's okay. You're safe."

She didn't move, but she didn't bolt either. I eased in beside her and gently ran a hand along her trembling back. Her fur was silky and warm. She shook like a leaf in a thunderstorm. Poor thing. She must have witnessed the entire episode with her owner. How much did she understand? How scared she must be. After a moment, I slid my hand underneath her and picked her up. She curled into my arms with a little sigh that broke my heart.

"What are you going to do with her?" Nick asked.

I blinked. Good question. "I don't really know. But I can't just leave her here like lost luggage." The place was eerily deserted. No officials, no show people, just us and a janitor pushing a broom like it was the only thing between him and clocking out. The rings and judges' tables had been torn down and removed either before or during the time I'd been occupied with Mrs. Blankenship. The only items remaining in the area were Mrs. Blankenship's portable table, her chair, and two crates. And her coffee thermos, lying sideways and still leaking onto the floor.

Remembering that I'd seen the woman brushing out a long-haired Chihuahua, I glanced in the crates to see if it was in one of them. But they were both empty.

"Nick, she had another dog. A long-haired

Chihuahua."

"I'll look around." He got to his feet and began searching the now cavernous building. There were only so many places an animal could hide. Still, Chihuahuas didn't take up much room and could squeeze in anywhere.

"Sir, have you seen a loose dog?" he asked the janitor, but the man shook his head. "It's tiny, a Chihuahua."

"Sorry, but I'll keep my eyes open."

Meanwhile, since it appeared that no one was coming back for Evangelina Rose, I supposed I'd have to take her with me. "Sweetie, let's get you settled in your crate. Then I guess you're going home with me."

I wondered how Sierra would react to a temporary roommate. I gently eased the wee dog out of my arms into one of the crates, where she cowered in the back, a trembling ball of fur. I folded up Mrs. Blankenship's table and chair, leaning them against the back wall, unsure what the proper etiquette was for handling the belongings of someone who might—or might not—be deceased.

I reached for the coffee thermos, then paused. Screwing the cap on, I tucked it under my arm and headed back to the veterinary station to finish packing up my stuff, the crate holding Evangelina Rose in my other hand.

Nick joined me a few moments later. "No sign of the other dog. I even looked in both restrooms."

My heart squeezed with worry. Had the other dog escaped in all the confusion? I thought about how easy it would have been for Evangelina Rose to slip out unnoticed. I wondered where Mr. Wigglesworth had gone. To the hospital, perhaps?

"I sure hope it turns up." I bent to lift a box.

"I'm sure it will be okay," Nick said, although he didn't sound convinced. "Let me help you with that." Nick took the box from my hands like a pack mule with good manners. He also grabbed the handle of my folding exam table and then nodded at the thermos. "What's that?"

"It's Mrs. Blankenship's. I don't know why I picked it up." I tucked it into the supply box he held, then led the way to my Sierra pick-up, carrying the crate and my controlled drug box.

"Looks like we're the last to leave," said Nick as he settled my gear into the truck bed while I secured Evangelina Rose in the front seat.

The sky had become a soft, shifting canvas of colors, with the sinking sun casting a warm, golden glow fading into deep oranges and muted pinks. Wisps of clouds caught the last light with fiery hues. A soft breeze skittered across the parking lot, sending dry leaves scurrying.

I brushed a strand of hair away from my eyes. "Thanks for all your help today. I really appreciate it. And especially the free food."

He grinned, but the grin fell just short of his eyes, which searched mine with a dark intensity that made my heart jump. "Despite everything, I had a good time today."

"Yeah, me too. Although I could have done without the grand finale." I bit my lip. "I really do hope Mrs. Blankenship is okay. Even if she will most certainly accuse me of stealing her show dog."

Nick laughed. "She'll probably sue you."

I shrugged. "Wouldn't surprise me. As the saying goes, 'no good deed goes unpunished.'"

We both stood awkwardly, maintaining the silence. Neither of us seemed to want to leave, but there was nothing more to say or do.

Finally, Nick cleared his throat. "So, are you hungry? I could buy you something besides a hot dog."

My heart leapt before reason caught up. "I'd love to, but I should get home. I don't want to leave Evangelina Rose in the car. Besides, my dog, Sierra, has been alone all day. She tends to sulk if I don't report in."

He nodded. "Okay. I understand. I enjoyed meeting you, Amy." He started to back away.

Wait! Wait! Wait! "But I'll take a rain check." The words flew out of my mouth, stopping him in his tracks. I dug through my purse for my business card, wrote my cell number on the back in readable print, and handed it to him. "Call me?"

His eyes lit up. "I will. Goodnight, Amy. Drive safe."

"You, too." I climbed into the cab and started the engine. He waited until I pulled out before getting into his van. Like a gentleman. Or a man who suspected I might hit a curb on my way out.

As I drove home, I reflected on the bizarre day and the strangeness of its ending. What would people say when they found out about Mildred Blankenship? How many would secretly suspect karma had finally caught up to her?

Then, an icy shiver skittered up my spine as a thought flashed through my brain.

What if it hadn't been karma . . . or a medical

issue?

What if someone had murdered Mrs. Blankenship?

Chapter Seven

The thought gnawed at me all night like a teething Chihuahua. How many people had I heard at the dog show say they wanted to kill Mrs. Blankenship? A dozen? Twenty? Okay, maybe just three. And people often said things they didn't mean literally when they were angry. But still, dog people can get weird.

I didn't want to think that someone would actually be so upset with Mrs. Blankenship that they would murder her, but I couldn't shake the image of someone offing her. My imagination was probably in overdrive, fueled by too many detective novels and an unhealthy amount of caffeine.

I sighed, flung the covers back, and swung my feet over the side of the bed onto the cold floor to check on Evangelina Rose. When I'd brought her home earlier, Sierra didn't know what to make of the itty-bitty creature. She wore a puzzled expression that said, *Surely, this isn't one of* my *kind, although it sort of smells like another dog.*

Evangelina Rose had refused to eat, drink, or make eye contact, opting to remain huddled in the back of her crate. I'd finally coaxed her out to do her business in the backyard, but the second we came inside, she bolted back to her crate like I was trying to sell her insurance. My heart went out to the little orphan. For all Mrs. Blankenship's faults—and they were many—her dog must have loved her. That's the thing about dogs. They love you even when you're a nightmare in orthopedic sandals.

I padded into the living room, guided by the faint glow from the hall nightlight shaped like a smiling cat. My gaze swept over Sierra, snoring peacefully in her bed. I knelt to peek into the crate and froze.

Evangelina Rose had disappeared. Oh no! If by some miracle, Mrs. Blankenship had survived, and I lost her dog . . . Well, I'd probably have to join the Witness Protection Program.

"Okay, okay, get a hold of yourself," I whispered to myself since I was the only one listening. "She's got to be somewhere. She didn't just evaporate into thin air."

But with a creature that size, she could've wedged herself anywhere, and I might not find her doggy skeleton until a year from next spring. I knew she wouldn't come if I called. But I couldn't go back to sleep until I attempted to find her.

I checked under and behind all the furniture and even in the closets in case she'd managed to flatten herself and crawl underneath the doors. Nothing.

Finally, I flipped the light on—although why I'd been afraid to wake Sierra before now, I couldn't rationalize. Movement from Sierra's bed caught my eye. A domed-shaped little head popped up, along with Sierra's blockhead. A warm rush of emotion swirled through my chest at the sight of Evangelina Rose snuggled up next to my mutt, one of Sierra's front paws curled protectively around her tiny body.

Sierra's sleepy-eyed expression said, *What? She was cold.*

"Sorry," I whispered. "Go back to sleep."

I switched off the light and tiptoed back to bed, a smile pulling on my lips. If Mrs. Blankenship could see her prized Chihuahua spooning with my mutt, she would keel over. Assuming she wasn't already dead.

My alarm mercifully cut into a nightmare I was having about the ordeal from the day before. Tempting as it was to face plant into my pillow, I had a children's Sunday school class to teach, and God frowns on absent teachers without good reason. I dragged my weary body from my warm bed and made my way into the living room, where Sierra greeted me with a full-body wag. Evangelina Rose stared out at me through her huge eyes as she lounged contentedly in Sierra's massive bed like royalty.

"Up and at 'em, girls. Let's go hit the lawn."

Sierra bounded to the kitchen door, but Evangelina Rose remained rooted to her spot. I scooped her up and deposited her on the dew-covered grass, where she tiptoed through it like she was auditioning for *Swan Lake* and couldn't put her paws completely flat. She finally did her business and scurried back to the patio.

I brought both dogs back inside and started my coffee maker, pondering what to feed Evangelina Rose. She had turned up her nose at Sierra's kibble the evening before, and I could only guess what she usually dined on. Filet mignon? Probably something that involved truffles and garnish.

I made a mental note to pick up some canned food

on my way home from church. For now, I decided to scramble an egg for her. Ordinarily, I didn't go to all this trouble for my own breakfast, let alone a dog's, but desperate times and all that.

Since I was making an egg for Evangelina Rose, I decided to forgo my usual bowl of cold cereal and scramble another egg for myself. Eat healthy for a change. I let Evangelina Rose's egg cool while I stood in the kitchen and gobbled down my own, remembering I'd skipped dinner last night. The thought of dinner made me think of Nick, and I felt a goofy grin lifting my cheeks. At least, I guess it was goofy. I wasn't near a mirror to confirm my suspicion. No matter; there wasn't anyone around to see me, thank goodness, in my ratty T-shirt and shorts, with my hair sticking up in all directions.

"Here you go, Evangelina Rose," I said, placing a saucer on the floor with her egg. The Chihuahua didn't budge from her spot in Sierra's bed, so I took the dish to her and set it down in front of her nose.

Sierra shot me a look that said, *What the heck? I never get breakfast in bed.*

"I know," I told my dog. "But she's had a hard time. She needs a little spoiling."

Sierra stuck her nose in the air and skulked away.

I sat cross-legged next to the bed, fingering the egg and holding it out to the wee dog. "Come on, baby, eat just a bite." I swear, if she didn't eat it, *I* would. I was still hungry, and the egg smelled good.

Evangelina Rose sniffed at the offering and then deemed to taste a smidgeon. "That's it. Good girl." She looked at me with those enormous, sad eyes and ate another bite. "Keep going, Evangel . . . You know what? If you're going to be stuck here with me for a while, I can't keep calling you by that long name. What if you run into the road and I yell, "Stop, Evangelina Rose! You'll be a grease spot before the first syllable leaves my mouth."

I thought for a moment. "How about 'Evie'?"

Now, I might have been imagining things, but I thought I saw a twinkle in her eye. The dog must have disliked her name as much as I did. Not that Evangelina Rose wasn't a pretty name, but it seemed somewhat inappropriate for a canine of her size. Still, I knew that show dogs often had extensive names. Maybe in her everyday existence, she went by "Evie."

She daintily nibbled a few more bites, and tempted as I was to eat the rest for her, I decided to forgo finishing a dog's breakfast. Besides, I was running late, and teaching about Jonah and the big fish wasn't going to teach itself.

When I returned home, juggling my oversized purse, Bible, Sunday school materials, and a plastic bag full of canned dog food, the last thing I expected was a police car in my driveway and two officers on my porch.

What on earth? Had Evie howled nonstop since I left the house, disturbing the neighbors? I didn't hear any noise, not even Sierra's deep woofs.

"Can I help you?" I asked, walking up the front steps, trying not to drop anything.

The officers turned. "Are you Dr. Amy Dixon?" the taller, more intimidating of the two asked.

"Yes," I said hesitantly.

"May we come in and speak with you for a few minutes?"

My heart did a little backflip. Why did the police want to talk to me? If I said no, would I be in trouble? I looked from one man to the other, but they gave nothing away.

"Uh, yeah, I guess so."

I squeezed between them and fumbled through my purse with a shaky hand, unable to snag my key.

"Here, would you mind holding this?" I shoved all my paraphernalia into the arms of the less intimidating policeman so I could dig more deeply into my bag. Why did I always drop my keys into the nether regions of my purse instead of taking the time to secure them in an easy-to-find place, like the conveniently situated outside zipper pocket? I finally emerged with the keys and opened the door.

Sierra gave a half-hearted "woof" and then wagged her tail furiously at the unexpected visitors. Evie stared at the intruders from the safety of Sierra's bed, with huge, unblinking eyes, her body trembling.

"Where do you want me to put this?" asked the officer holding all my stuff.

"Oh. Sorry." I grabbed everything from his arms and deposited it on the coffee table. Should I invite them to sit down? It felt rather awkward just standing in the doorway.

"May we sit down?" asked the bigger cop.

"Yes, of course." I gestured to the sofa and two end chairs.

The first officer, the large, intimidating man, settled into one of the end chairs. His belly overlapped his belt as he folded into the seat, and he kept his stern eyes on mine. The second man, younger and smaller, sank into the end of the couch, leaned forward with his elbows resting on his knees, and shot me a sympathetic smile. Were they going to play "good cop, bad cop?"

I lowered myself to the edge of the other end chair and again divided my attention between the two, who sat on opposite sides of the room. My heart banged against my ribs so loudly I knew they could hear it.

"I'm Officer Barrows, and this is Officer Lang," Stern Cop said. "We're here about the death of Mildred Blankenship."

My breath caught. So, she did die. Not that I hadn't expected the news. But a sadness came over me at the confirmation.

"Oh, I'm sorry to hear that. I did CPR on her forever, but I never got a pulse."

Nice Cop cleared his throat. "We understand you had an altercation with her earlier in the day."

My heart plummeted into my stomach. Okay, maybe he wasn't so nice after all. How did they know that?

"I . . . I wouldn't call it an altercation. She was upset because her regular veterinarian wasn't there yesterday."

"Mr. Wigglesworth said you refused to treat her dog."

"*What*?" I blinked. Why the little weasel! He'd completely twisted things. "No, that's not true. She refused *me*. She didn't *want* me to treat her dog. She kept insisting I call her regular veterinarian to come in, but I wouldn't do that because he was in the emergency room with a kidney stone and I was just filling in for him as a favor and . . ." *Stop rambling.*

The two exchanged glances, and the older one winced. Apparently, he'd fought the rocky battle of kidney stones.

"Okay, so what happened?" Lang turned on the warm, fuzzy voice.

"Nothing!" My voice came out too shrill. *Calm down, Amy.* I sucked in a long breath and counted to three in my head. "She complained about me not calling the other veterinarian to Mr. Wigglesworth, and he came over to try to straighten things out. Her dog had a broken toenail."

Barrows rolled his eyes.

Sensing an ally, I pounced on him. "Yes, a broken toenail. Before I could do anything, a groomer came over, took the dog from her, and clipped off the broken edge." At their blank looks, I felt the need to add, "It didn't even bleed." Still blank stares. "That's it. That was the whole story. She was upset because her regular veterinarian wasn't available, and she made a scene."

Lang leaned in. "Then why did she threaten to report you to the veterinary medical board?"

My eyes grew as round as Evie's. What had Mr. Wigglesworth told them? The man practically had me strangling her with my stethoscope.

I forced my expression into something between calm and not homicidal and took a moment to gather my thoughts. "Look, Mrs. Blankenship was a professional bully. She liked to throw her weight around—and she had plenty to throw." I chuffed out what I hoped sounded like a "give me a break" laugh. "But seriously, Officer, do you think the board would yank my license over a broken toenail? They'd laugh, throw the complaint into the trash, and maybe send me a sympathy card."

That response got the tiniest twitch of a smirk from Barrows.

Another thought hit me with the suddenness of a runaway train. Why the interrogation? Had Mrs. Blankenship died of something other than natural causes?

"Wait," I said slowly, "didn't Mrs. Blankenship die of a heart attack or something?"

The officers exchanged more glances. Oh boy.

The Barrows shook his head grimly. "No, she did not. She was poisoned."

Every cell in my body screeched to a halt. *Poisoned!* Oh. My. Goodness. My worst fear had just been confirmed. I had spent the day at the dog show with a murderer! I needed caffeine. And maybe a paper bag to breathe into.

Barrows leaned forward, his eyes narrowed. "You didn't ask what she was poisoned with."

My heart, which had settled in my stomach, now climbed into my throat. Why should they expect me to ask? What did any of this have to do with me? Why would I . . . Oh, no. This *was* about me!

I tried to push the word from my throat around my heart. "What?"

"Phenobarbital." His eyes bore into mine.

My heart stopped altogether, and I feared one of them would have to administer CPR to *me*. I felt the blood drain from my face.

"Did you have phenobarbital with you yesterday?"

"Well . . . yes," I stammered, "but—"

"Where do you keep your controlled drugs, Dr.

Dixon?"

Panic tap-danced across my spine. I had messed up again. I should have taken the controlled drug box back to the clinic and emptied the contents into the wall safe. But with all the commotion and having Evie with me, I'd neglected to do so. Ordinarily, it wouldn't have been a big deal, as I could have returned the controlled drugs this afternoon or even in the morning.

Don't look guilty. I tried to channel a confident, responsible medical professional. Not *I totally shoved my bag of narcotics and tranquilizers under my bed like a teenager hiding dirty magazines from his parents.*

"I keep them in a locked box when I go on house or farm calls," I said, trying not to sweat visibly. "Otherwise, they're locked up at my clinic."

"Do you have your box with you now?"

Busted. "Yes."

"May we see it?"

I pushed off the edge of the chair and walked on rubbery legs to my bedroom, where I'd stashed the box under the bed next to a pair of mismatched socks and a squeaky toy. Yeah, not the best hiding place, but then, nobody had ever broken into my house looking for drugs. Yet.

I returned to the living room and set the box on the coffee table right next to my Bible.

"Would you open it, please?"

Of course. Right after I remember where I put the keys. I located them mixed in with my scattered lesson notes from Jonah and dutifully unlocked the box.

Lang opened the lid and riffled through the contents until he pulled out the bottle of 1.5-grain phenobarbital. He shot a grim look at his partner, then unscrewed the cap and turned the bottle upside down.

Empty.

Chapter Eight

"Mr. Granger, this is Dr. Amy Dixon. We met at the dog show yesterday, remember? You said if I ever needed your services . . ." Panic crept into my voice. How could this be happening? I blinked wildly, half-expecting the room to spin into a surreal nightmare. A crazed laugh burst out of me. "Well, ha ha, you see, I'm at the police station, and they think I killed Mrs. Blankenship."

"Have they charged you with anything?"

His calm, no-nonsense voice dialed my hysteria back a notch.

I took a shaky breath. "No, but they brought me in for questioning." The words clung to me with a mix of disbelief and dread.

"Have you told them anything?" he pressed.

My thoughts swirled in a discombobulated mess. What had I told the police? Anything incriminating? I thought back to all those crime dramas I'd binge-watched. If the accused talked too much, the cops would let him hang himself.

"I . . . I don't remember." How pitiful I sounded.

"Have they read you your rights?"

Had they? I couldn't remember. Panic had completely erased my brain.

"I don't remember."

"Don't say another word. Which precinct are you at?"

"I don't know." I looked sideways at Lang. "Which precinct is this?"

"The ninth," he said, clearly miffed because I'd insisted on calling a lawyer. I knew how *that* looked, too. If you called a lawyer, it automatically made you look guilty and removed any chance of a plea deal.

A plea deal! Oh! My goodness! My whole future flashed before me. I looked terrible in orange. Who would take care of Sierra? And Evie? I was a trusted veterinarian, for Pete's sake. People who loved animals didn't go around murdering people, did they? How could they possibly think I could do such a thing? I'd tried to save the dreadful woman, after all. How did I get sucked into this horrific situation?

Breathe, Amy.

"Dr. Dixon, are you there?" Mr. Granger's voice broke in, my lifeline to rescuing me from this absurd misunderstanding.

"Yes, sorry. The ninth."

"Don't say another word," he repeated. "I'm on my way."

A mixture of relief and unreality washed over me. I swallowed around the dryness in my throat and shot a glance at Lang, who still glowered at me with unspoken judgment, making me feel even more like a desperate extra in a bad crime show.

"He's on his way," I said, like I expected Lang to be ecstatic over that information, despite the small amount of comfort it gave me.

He opened his mouth as if he were going to say something, then clamped it shut. He got up and exited the room, leaving me alone in the interrogation room to stew in my own anxiety. I knew how this worked, too. They left suspects to rot for hours in these rooms while they cranked up the heat and spied on them from behind a one-way mirror.

My mental loop replayed the details. They'd informed me that the phenobarbital had been put into Mrs. Blankenship's coffee, and I'd voluntarily surrendered her thermos I'd picked up the night before. Didn't that say something about my willingness to cooperate? Still, I needed a miracle to look less like the guilty party.

What could I do to appear less guilty? Get up and walk around nonchalantly? Stay glued in my hard, wooden seat with my hands folded in my lap in prayer? Scroll through Facebook? Nope, they'd confiscated my phone when they brought me in. At least they'd allowed me to keep my purse after a thorough search to be sure I didn't have a concealed ice pick.

I took a drink of the bottled water they'd offered me when I first came in, choking it down around the burning lump of terror lodged in my throat, and tried to think rationally.

Think, Amy, think. The silent chant from my brain exhorted me to reason this dilemma out.

Other than the fact that Mrs. Blankenship had obviously been poisoned with my phenobarbital, what evidence did they really have? I'd already explained how my drug box had inadvertently been left unlocked when I'd been called away to attend to an emergency.

Careless, yes, but not self-incriminating. I mean, seriously, if I'd wanted to kill the woman, would I have deliberately used drugs from my own box? How stupid would that be? My brain conjured up a number of other ways I could have slipped poison into her coffee without pointing to myself. Then, the fact that I was even considering other ways of doing the woman in stopped me cold. My mind didn't normally roam around in such dark places. Being in this place had made me unhinged.

Think, Amy. The phenobarbital had to have been put into the coffee thermos when Mrs. Blankenship was away from her table. The only time I knew of when she'd not been seated in her chair was when she was berating me for not being Dr. Collins, and when she was in the show ring. The show ring! Nick and I had watched the Chihuahua competition. He was my alibi! I had to get hold of him. But how? I'd given him my card, but he hadn't given me his. What if he didn't call? Panic sent my heart thumping again.

Of course, I couldn't *prove* the phenobarbital had been slipped into the coffee during the time Mrs. Blankenship showed Evie. She could have left her thermos unattended at any time I wasn't privy to. And did she show Evie before or after I'd left my drug box unattended? Confusion clouded my memory.

A bead of sweat trickled down my temple. Was it getting hotter in here, or was my internal panic heating things up? I resisted the urge to wipe my brow, turn around, and stare into the mirror with the question on my lips.

After what seemed like an eternity, the door opened, and Mr. Granger stepped into the room, accompanied by Lang, who wore a scowl. As soon as I saw the lawyer, all my composure evaporated, and I crumpled into a tearful heap, wondering how I'd gone from broken toenails to felony suspicion. I'm sure my running mascara made me look like a deranged raccoon.

"I'd like to question my client privately," Mr. Granger declared, his tone all business.

Lang flattened his lips and tilted his chin toward the door, where he led us to a smaller room off to the side.

Mr. Granger laid an expensive leather briefcase on the battered wooden table and took a seat. He flipped open the top and extracted a yellow legal pad, pen, and a wad of tissues, which he thrust into my trembling hand.

"Start at the beginning."

In a frantic rush, I recounted everything I could to the best of my ability, with him nodding and interrupting every so often to clarify a point.

"So," he said, laying down his pen and folding his hands on the table, "from what I can tell, all they have is circumstantial evidence. Tell me about the other people who had run-ins with Mrs. Blankenship."

I racked my brain, and images of the Battleship's unjustly persecuted characters sprang to my memory. Besides all the ugly comments I'd heard muttered in the crowd, I'd observed at least four heated arguments. I struggled to recall the names.

"Um, there was this one woman who was furious because a puppy she'd bought from Mrs. Blankenship had seizures and she couldn't breed him. Mrs. Blankenship blew her off. I heard her say, 'One day, you'll get yours.'" I rubbed my aching forehead. "What was her name?" The woman's face flashed in my mind as I replayed that scene. "Trudy. I think her name was Trudy."

"Do you have a last name?"

Did I? "I don't think so. But I bet Nick would know."

"Nick, the man who sold concessions?"

"Yes, remember I told you we were together on and off during the day."

"Why would he know?"

"Because his family has worked the dog show circuit for years. He knew everybody."

Mr. Granger nodded and scribbled more notes. "Okay, who else?"

I remembered another disgruntled woman. "Well, there was another lady who accused Mrs. Blankenship of bribing the judge when her dog took second place instead of first. I believe I heard Mrs. Blankenship call her Darlene. But I don't know her last name."

"Darlene." He wrote the name on his pad.

"She told Mrs. Blankenship that she should watch her back. And then a guy named Billings . . . What was his first name? Um, Martin, that's it. He was a menacing guy in dire need of anger management. I distinctly heard him say she would regret what she did. She owed him ten thousand dollars for dog training, but refused to pay because she said he didn't do his job correctly."

Mr. Granger whistled. "That's a lot of motive."

A spark of hope ignited from the realization that lots of people wanted the woman dead. Maybe suspicion would deflect onto someone besides me.

"Oh, and another woman said she'd kill Mrs. Blankenship for spreading lies about her breeding program. She lost a puppy sale because of Mrs. Blankenship."

"Do you remember the woman's name?"

Ooh. I squinted my eyes. I remembered the hideous tight dress and clunky heels. "Joanna!" I said, a smile spreading over my face. The smile slipped as soon as it had appeared. "No last name, I'm afraid."

"It's okay. We can get those later. For now, let me go tell the cops they either need to charge you or let you go."

My blood froze. Would they throw me in the slammer?

My expression must have shown on my face because his features softened. "Don't worry. They don't have enough to hold you." He strode purposefully to the door and threw it open. "Officer Lang? We're done here."

The police officer returned to the room, and Mr. Granger went for the jugular. "Do you have any eyewitnesses or video surveillance showing my client putting the drug into the coffee?"

Lang shifted his feet. "No. There are no surveillance cameras in that part of the fairgrounds."

"What about surveillance cameras in the area where the drug box was kept?"

"No, I'm afraid not," the policeman admitted.

"Then anyone could have slipped in and taken the pills while my client was distracted with the emergency. Isn't that possible?"

"It's possible, but—"

"Do you have any proof that my client intended to

harm the victim?"

A pause ensued, then Lang mumbled, "Not directly, but the phenobarbital came from her drug box. And she 'just so happened' to take the coffee thermos with her. Plus, the threat of the veterinary board complaint."

Mr. Granger waved his hand in a dismissive manner similar to the one Mrs. Blankenship had perfected. "Mrs. Blankenship had public altercations with several people at the dog show that day. My client wasn't the only one she clashed with. I have here the names of four people who were angry with her. A couple even made threats against her."

That got Lang's attention. His eyes flew to the legal pad in Mr. Granger's hand. "Who?"

"If you'd do your job, I wouldn't have to do it for you." Mr. Granger tore off the top sheet from his legal pad and passed it to the policeman. "It doesn't look like you've done much of an investigation."

Lang took the paper and studied it for a moment. "Three of these people have no last names."

My attorney let out an exasperated sigh. "It shouldn't be too hard to track them down. Isn't that part of your job?" He made a show of checking his watch. "Now, this is where we're at. You have no evidence of my client's involvement in this crime. You're suggesting Dr. Dixon used a controlled substance with her name on it in a public place with a crowd of witnesses and no clear motive." He shook his head as if he found the whole scenario absurd, which it was. "That's not just unlikely, it's illogical."

"She didn't secure the drug box."

"Negligence isn't murder. Unless you've got actual

footage of Dr. Dixon putting pills into that woman's coffee, you have no case." Granger made a show of turning his back on the officer and stowing his legal pad back into his briefcase. Once he'd snapped the case closed, he turned back slowly and said, "Are you prepared to officially charge Dr. Dixon?"

Lang cast a long, distasteful look at me. And to think, in the beginning, I'd thought him to be the "good" cop. "Not at this time."

"Good, then we're out of here. Come, Dr. Dixon."

Granger placed his reassuring hand on the small of my back and indicated for me to precede him out the door, for which I was grateful. From this distance, I could feel the fiery darts from Lang's eyes landing on our backs, and Granger's back was closer and broader. I guess lawyers had thicker skins than veterinarians.

"Don't leave town, Dr. Dixon," Lang called after us. "We may have more questions for you."

Yikes! Did cops really say that?

I stopped briefly and said over my shoulder, "I have no intention of going anywhere, Officer Lang. I have a clinic to run."

With that, we disappeared down the corridor, a mixture of absurdity, relentless panic, and the slightest glimmer of triumph propelling us forward into a chaos that was equal parts legal slapstick and genuine terror.

As we reached the wide-open parking lot, the suffocating confines of the police station seemed like a bad dream I'd finally outrun. I'd never considered myself claustrophobic before—until now. The thought of prison wrapped icy tendrils around my heart. If I were locked up, I'd literally climb the walls like a cockroach.

I turned to Mr. Granger and released the breath I hadn't realized I'd been holding. "Thank you. I've never been in a situation like this before." *Well, gee, I should hope not!* What would my church say? They probably wouldn't condone a felon teaching preschoolers.

He chuckled. "I'm happy to help. Don't worry. They don't have anything on you. They're just shaking the tree to see what falls out."

"What do I do now?"

He patted my shoulder with the confidence of a man who'd gotten hundreds of potential felons freed. "Don't do anything. Don't say anything more to the police unless I'm with you."

I nodded. How was I supposed to carry on as though nothing had happened? And despite Mr. Granger's assurances of "happy to help," I wasn't naïve enough to believe that his services would be completely covered by what I'd done for his dog yesterday.

How much did defense lawyers cost? I would have to treat a lot of soft tissue injuries to cover his fee.

Chapter Nine

I remained huddled on the sofa, hugging a pillow as though it were a life raft, trying to untangle the mess of the past twenty-four hours. Sierra, my unofficial support canine, sensing my distress, did her best to comfort me by snuggling close and licking my face every so often. Evie remained in Sierra's bed, eyeing me with a mixture of bewilderment and unconcern. Her world had been knocked off its axis, too.

How could I break this news to my parents? The thought made my stomach churn. They would be mortified to learn their overachieving, hot-shot veterinarian daughter was a murder suspect. I'd put that off for now.

As if I conjured my parents by telepathy, the phone rang. My heart lurched. My parents would instantly know something was wrong, and they wouldn't stop digging until they'd ferreted out the truth, probably within seconds of me saying "hello." They were like bloodhounds tracking a scent when I tried to hide anything from them.

I snatched my phone from the end table and let out a breath. Not my parents. A number I didn't recognize flashed on the screen. Probably a telemarketer. I hoped so. I needed to lash out at somebody, and who better than an intrusive telemarketer?

"Hello," I snapped.

After a heavy pause, a familiar voice piped up. "Uh, Amy? Did I catch you at a bad time?"

Relief flooded through me as though the dam barely holding my emotions in check had burst. "Nick!" I cried. Then, I literally began to cry.

"Amy, what's wrong?" Concern colored his tone, making me feel even worse.

For a moment, I couldn't speak. Finally, I blurted out, "The police think I killed Mrs. Blankenship!"

"*What?*" His voice rose an octave. "Why on earth would they think that?"

Between bouts of ugly sobs, I recounted the whole sordid chain of events that had transpired that afternoon.

"That is ridiculous," he said when I'd finished.

"As far as they're concerned, I'm the prime suspect. I don't think they're seriously going to look at anybody else," I said, my voice shaking with terror and disbelief.

"Then we'll just have to look *for* them," he said, resolution in his voice.

"Wh . . . what do you mean?" I asked, sniffling. I wiped my runny nose on my sleeve.

"I mean, we may have to investigate ourselves."

His brash words cut my tears off like a faucet. "Us? But Nick, I'm a veterinarian, and you're an insurance adjuster slash hot dog vendor. We're not private detectives. We don't have the experience or the knowledge to conduct a police investigation."

He countered with a sly laugh. "I didn't say we would conduct a police investigation. In fact, we may get better results if we're *not* professionals."

"But how? Where would we even start?" The chaos in my life suddenly grew stronger, if that were possible.

"Let's start with the four suspects you mentioned—the ones you observed who had an ax to grind with the late, great, monstrous Battleship."

I groaned. "But I don't even know the last names of three of those people."

Nick's voice took on a conspiratorial tone. "That's where I can help. I've known Darlene McDougal and Joana Papadopoulos for years. Well, not known them personally, exactly, but I know who they are."

"What about Trudy?"

"Sorry, I don't know who she is. But we can start with the other three. I say let's talk to Martin Billings first. Of the four, he seems like the most likely suspect. He's volatile, plus there's the issue of a ten-thousand-dollar debt."

I laughed nervously. This was so not funny. "So, what are we going to say to him? Uh, excuse me, Mr. Billings, did you happen to kill Mildred Blankenship?"

Nick chuckled. "Not exactly. But I have an idea. We'll call him tomorrow and make an appointment to talk to him about dog training. He obviously needs the money. He'll jump at the chance to talk to us."

"Nick, it's not that I don't appreciate you trying to help, but couldn't this be dangerous?"

"Not if we play it smart. All we're going to do is try to get him to open up to us about the Battleship. See what he knows. Don't you trust your detective instincts?"

"What detective instincts?"

"Come on, Amy, you play detective every day when some client comes in and says, 'I don't know what's wrong with Fluffy.' Fluffy doesn't exactly volunteer that information, right?"

I drew in a long breath. "I don't know. That's different. That's not dangerous."

"Unless Fluffy bites you."

"Nick—"

"Look, you said the police weren't doing anything. Do you want to get off the police's radar?"

"Yes, of course, but—"

"Then we've got to take matters into our own hands." His tone was a mix of determination and mischief.

Doubt nibbled at my common sense.

"I'll track down his number and see if we can meet with him tomorrow night."

The prospect of spending the evening with Nick outweighed the risk of being with a murder suspect.

"All right," I agreed. What had I just gotten myself into?

I walked into work the next day, determined to keep my chin up and my mouth shut, hoping to go about my usual routine and pretend like nothing had happened.

"Amy!" cried Tess, my technician and good friend, the minute I stepped over the threshold. "Did you hear what happened at the dog show on Saturday?"

So much for keeping things quiet.

I stopped, closed my eyes, and inhaled sharply, the scent of wet dog and flea shampoo hitting me like aromatherapy, sending calming chemicals to my brain.

"A breeder was *murdered!*" Tess went on. "Can you imagine? At a dog show?"

There was no point in playing dumb. Tess had a sixth sense for gossip and a seventh for secrets, and if I didn't spill, she'd find out anyway—and be personally offended I hadn't told her first.

"Yes, I know. I was there."

"What?" Her eyes widened. "Why?"

"I got called in for Dr. Collins, who was in the emergency room with a kidney stone," I said, suddenly resenting his inner plumbing. If his renal system had picked any other day to implode, I'd have spent Saturday doing something boring, like cleaning out my refrigerator and vacuuming dog hair from my carpet. Instead, I got a front-row seat to Mrs. Blankenship's final curtain call.

I might have read the story in the paper or heard it on the news and thought, "Gee, that's too bad," and gone on with my life none the wiser. It's downright scary how a tiny twist of fate can reroute your whole life. In my case, life behind bars.

Tess' excitement kicked into high gear. "So, what happened? Did you see anything?"

Oh, boy, did I. I glanced around, but nobody else seemed to be within earshot, so I pulled her into the office, shut the door, and unloaded everything. Her expression morphed from morbid curiosity to disbelief to horror.

"I can't believe it," she said for the dozenth time.

"Yeah, well, that makes two of us." I sighed. "So, if the police come and haul me off in handcuffs, promise me you'll take care of Sierra."

"Oh, Amy, that's not going to happen. They'll find the real killer."

"I'm not so sure about that. That's why Nick and I are going to do a little investigating on our own." I filled her in on our brilliant, totally ill-advised plans for tonight.

Her mouth dropped open. "That doesn't sound like such a good idea."

"We'll be careful," I said, trying to convince both of us. The fact was, I didn't have a clue how we were going to get Martin Billings to talk. "In the meantime, this stays between us. Business as usual around here. Got it?"

Worry lines creased her forehead. "Okay, but if you don't turn up for work tomorrow, I'm going to the police and spill my guts."

"Deal." I forced a smile. "Now, let's get to work. I need something to take my mind off this mess. Something routine. Something that doesn't involve corpses. What have we got going on this morning?"

She seemed to struggle to shift gears, then finally said, "You have three neuters on the surgery schedule for this morning before appointments start at ten."

I rubbed my hands together. "Great. There's nothing like a neuter to lift my spirits."

"I'll find Alaina and start sedating the surgeries."

Twenty minutes later, I stood gowned, capped, masked, and gloved with my scalpel poised over the surgical site of my first neuter patient. Tess stood on the other side of the table, all business—until she glanced around and then leaned in close.

"Do you have a gun?" she whispered.

I raised my eyes. "Only a tranquilizer gun."

"Maybe you should take it with you."

I blew out a breath, which inflated my mask like a sad balloon, and fogged my surgical glasses. "Tess, I am not going to a meeting on the pretense of hiring a man to train my dog armed with a dart gun."

"Well, what if he attacks you?"

"He's not going to attack me. Mrs. B was killed by someone sneaking phenobarbital into her coffee, not by someone strangling her with their bare hands. Besides, Nick will be with me." I couldn't help the slight lilt that crept into my voice.

"Ah, yes, Nick." Her words carried a knowing tone, the smirk on her face leaving no doubt.

Heat flamed on my cheeks, which were conveniently covered by my mask. "It's not like that. Yet, anyway. I mean, I *think* he's interested in me, and I *hope* he's interested in me—"

"I'd say any guy who's willing to confront murderers with you is definitely interested."

I sighed. "I must admit, it's a rather unconventional first date."

"Let's just pray it's not your last date."

"Gee, thanks, Tess, that makes me feel so much better."

"Well, I'm concerned. So, sue me."

I groaned. "Please don't say 'sue me.' The old Battleship threatened everyone around her with lawsuits. Including me."

Tess snorted. "I guess you can forget about being sued. That's one court date she'll miss."

"Could we please change the subject? I've got work to do."

Chapter Ten

The morning mercifully passed uneventfully, except for one dog who woke up from surgery howling like a banshee. I don't know whether his dismay resulted from the loss of his manhood or simply a bad trip on anesthesia. Either way, I was used to noise from the kennel. It didn't even make me blink anymore.

At lunchtime, I slipped away to check on Sierra and Evie, whom I had left at home. To my surprise, Evie stood in Sierra's bed and greeted me with a tentative tail wag. I guess she'd realized with her owner out of the picture that I was now her meal ticket and potentially her emotional support human.

After letting them outside to do their business, I made myself a peanut butter and jelly sandwich and perused the news on my phone—big mistake.

The murder at the dog show made the headlines. I supposed that was to be expected since this was the most exciting event to happen in our small town since someone mistook the mayor's new drone (complete with festive Christmas lights) for a UFO and started a town-wide panic. The details remained sketchy, but one sentence made me choke on my sandwich—police say they have a likely suspect.

I coughed up grape jelly and took a swig of water, trying to steady my erratic heartbeat.

I tried to talk myself down. Surely, they weren't talking about me, right? Maybe they'd interviewed one of the four people Mr. Granger and I had helpfully tried to shift police attention to. My palms began to sweat, and I laid down my sandwich, no longer hungry.

I didn't know what to do. Call the police and politely ask, "Hi, quick question. Am I your prime suspect, or just your second favorite?" Should I call Mr. Granger and ask him to file . . . something? A motion? An injunction? A cease-and-desist-slandering-my-good-name order? Did the police have to mention me by name for him to take legal action?

Or should I pack up whatever I could in my truck, hit the road, and start over in Belize or some country without extradition?

No. That would make me look even *more* guilty, and I would never be able to clear my name. I needed to find the real killer. Fast. Especially if I wanted even the faintest shot at a future with Nick. Yes, I know—I was already imagining happily ever after with a man I'd just met, which would be difficult from a prison cell. But in all honesty, it had been a long time since I'd met anyone with whom I'd felt an instant connection. Someone who made my heart skip a beat. And certainly not with someone who looked like he'd walked out of a firefighter calendar and could actually carry on a conversation.

But then, the rational side of my brain reared its annoyingly logical head. What did I really know about Nick? Looking at the picture from a non-biased standpoint, for all I knew, Nick could have been the one to lace Mrs. Blankenship's coffee with barbiturates. Maybe I'd read him all wrong, and he was a secret serial killer with bodies in his basement. Sure, he was drop-dead handsome—perhaps a poor choice of words, given the circumstances—but so was Ted Bundy.

I pressed my hands to my pounding temples to unweave the mental spaghetti. Nick was *not* a serial killer. Probably. Besides, he had no vendetta against Mrs. Blankenship that I knew of. Unless he deliberately volunteered to work at the concession stand on his day off so he could get close to the woman. *Sure, Amy, and he just happened to know you would go off and leave your controlled drug box unattended, giving him the perfect opportunity to get rid of his nemesis while casting the blame on you.*

Letting my brain wander around loose by itself was not helping. I needed a leash for my thoughts. Didn't the Bible say something about taking every thought captive? But rounding my thoughts up and taking them captive at the moment was like herding cats. I needed to get back to work.

I threw myself into my routine—puppy vaccines, catfight abscesses, and a parakeet with a serious attitude problem. It almost helped quiet the panic—until I had to do a nail trim. That was when the emotional dam cracked. My hands started shaking like I'd downed six expressos, and Tess had to take over while I practiced deep breathing in my office like a yoga novice having a meltdown.

The intercom interrupted me. "Dr. Dixon?" came the voice of the receptionist.

"Yes?"

"Dr. Collins is on line one for you."

Oh great. Dr. Collins. I had to rein in my emotions before picking up the receiver and laying in to the man for having the audacity to pass a kidney stone last Saturday, leaving me to face felony charges.

I took one more deep breath, picked up the phone, and forced a cheerful tone into my voice. "Dr. Collins, I hope you're feeling better."

He chuckled. *Easy for him. He had an alibi for the time of Mrs. Blankenship's murder.* "Much better, thank you, although I could have sworn I was going to die on Saturday."

That would have made two of you.

"Listen, I just wanted to thank you for stepping in and covering for me on such short notice. I hope everything went okay."

I hesitated. How much did I really want to tell him?

"Well, as far as the veterinary duties went, I had no major problems. However . . ." I proceeded to inform him about Mrs. Blankenship's death, leaving out the part about murder and me being a suspect. The fewer people who knew, the better.

"Oh, how dreadful! Mildred Blankenship has been a client of mine for years." He chuckled again. "A tad high-maintenance, but she was a good breeder. And she always paid her bill."

I also left out the part about her insisting he come in to take care of Evie's toenail. He didn't need to know that his client valued Evie's pedicure over his renal crisis.

"I'm sorry," I said, for lack of anything better to say while trying not to cry over possible incarceration.

We made polite small talk for another couple of minutes, then hung up. I couldn't blame him for my predicament. He hadn't purposefully chosen to have a kidney stone and leave me to deal with a murder investigation. It was just bad luck.

Bad luck. Wrong place. Wrong time.

But one thing was certain. If I wanted to survive this, I needed to keep my head on straight. Or at least screwed on tighter than it was right now. So, I did what any responsible adult on the verge of a breakdown would do. I got back to work and hoped nobody noticed I was one loose thread away from unraveling.

Chapter Eleven

As the day wore to a close, my nerves began to tingle—whether from the looming undercover mission or the prospect of seeing Nick again, I couldn't say. I sure hope he had a plan because I had nothing. Nada.

I said goodnight to the clinic staff with what I hoped was casually routine and headed for my truck. Tess raced after me, cornering me in the parking lot, where she just stood staring at me.

"What?" I asked.

"I'm afraid I'll never see you again." Her lower lip wobbled.

I rolled my eyes. "Oh, for the love of . . . Tess, I'm not infiltrating a drug cartel. I'm just going to ask questions about training my dog. I'll be fine. I promise." Well, I couldn't truly promise I'd be fine. For all I knew, I could get T-boned by a semi-truck pulling into my driveway.

"But this guy could be a murderer!"

"I'll be sure to keep my coffee thermos with me at all times."

She flattened her lips. "It's not funny. Call me the minute you're home and tell me what happened."

"All right. I need to go. Nick is picking me up in

twenty minutes." And I needed to find my most flattering outfit—casual, mind you—and freshen my makeup.

A few minutes later, a knock on my door made me jump hard enough to spill the French roast I slurped to give me caffeine confidence down my shirt. Perfect. Nothing screams "girl trying to impress a guy" like a coffee stain on my favorite shirt.

I grabbed a jacket from the back of a chair and pulled it on as I headed for the door, hoping it would hide the stain and not clash with my outfit. Nick stood on the porch looking, annoyingly, like a man hadn't just spent the last hour worrying about his appearance.

"Ready?" he asked, flashing that smile that made my knees go weak.

"Remind me again why we're going to talk to Mr. Billings instead of, say, leaving this to the professionals?" I asked as I locked the door behind me and accompanied Nick to his car. I guess he only drove the catering van on jobs.

Nick opened the passenger door for me, which was charming and unnecessary, but I wasn't one to turn down chivalry.

"Because," he said, once I was buckled in and he'd started the engine, "the professionals seem more interested in you than in actual suspects. And Billings was one ticked-off dude. I would be, too, if I were out ten grand."

I nodded, tugging my jacket sleeves down over my shaking hands.

"Do we have a plan?"

"Yes," he said. "We pretend to be interested in his services. We ask questions. We listen. And we try not to accuse him of murder in the first sixty seconds."

"I'll aim for ninety," I muttered.

Nick chuckled. "Progress."

We drove in silence for a few miles, winding past farmland and fields peppered with dandelions and an occasional cow chewing thoughtfully as we passed. I stared out the window, watching the scenery blur by, but my mind wouldn't settle.

"What if he really didn't do anything?" I asked. "What if we're wrong?"

"We're not going to directly accuse the man of murder."

"And what if he did do it?"

He glanced at me, his eyes serious for once. "Then we'll figure out what to do next. Together."

I hated how my stomach did a tiny flip at that word. *Together.* It was the kind of thing that sounded nice in theory until one of you got thrown in jail, and the other ended up giving interviews on Dateline.

Nick's idea had us meeting with Mr. Billings at a quirky little training facility on the outskirts of town. We pulled up in front of a weathered-looking ranch house with a porch sagging under the weight of a very large, very disinterested bloodhound. A banner with paw prints and the words "Sit Happens" fluttered from a crooked pole out front, and a life-sized cutout of a Golden retriever in a graduation hat grinned at us near the door.

Several vehicles were parked helter-skelter across the yard. Great! A host of witnesses! Billings wouldn't try anything murderous in a group of people. Then, again, someone had done exactly that by spiking Mrs. Blankenship's coffee in the middle of a crowd.

Nick parked, turned off the engine, and glanced at me. "Ready to play undercover?"

"I'm already sweating, and I haven't even lied yet," I muttered, smoothing my hair.

"You'll be fine. Just follow my lead."

"Right," I said, feeling somewhat like a dog at the end of a leash. I took a deep breath and opened my car door. "Let's go see if Mr. Billings is feeling chatty."

Nick grinned. "After you, Dr. Dixon. Just try not to hit him with your stethoscope."

"No promises," I said as I stepped out of the car. "It's been a rough couple of days, and I may have to beat a confession out of him."

The sound of barks and whistles greeted us, and my eyes followed the sound to a fenced-in area on the side of the house where a pack of dogs and their humans trotted in laps under the barking orders of Mr. Billings. Clipboard in hand, whistle around his neck, he looked more like a drill sergeant than a dog trainer. He looked up as we approached and held up one finger for us to wait.

"Okay, that's it for today. Work on those 'sits' and 'downs' for next week." A couple of people hung back to exchange words with the trainer while the rest of the class filed out past us, with an assortment of dogs jumping and wagging their tails as if to say, *Did I do good?*

Finally, to my dismay, everyone departed, and we were alone with Mr. Billings. In the middle of nowhere.

The large man strode to us, all smiles and teeth like a used-car salesman—nothing like the furious, intimidating man from the dog show.

Nick held out his hand. "Nick Wyman. We spoke

on the phone about getting training for my girlfriend's dog."

Girlfriend! I almost swooned right on the spot.

Billings raised a brow at me. "Where's the dog?"

The dog? What dog? Weren't we talking about girlfriends?

Focus, Amy. I cleared my throat and tried to clear my head. "Uh, we didn't bring her with us. We wanted to learn more about your services first."

He nodded and turned up the charm. "What breed is she?"

I tried to pull off a laugh, but the sound came out more like a strangled goose honk. "That's a good question. She's probably got some hound dog mixed with Lab, and possibly some Boxer. Oh, and maybe Dachshund."

He blinked. "That's quite a combination."

"Well, you see, I don't really know for sure what she is. I found her by the side of the road. She's really smart, but I admit I'm way too soft with her. She needs some formal training."

"I see." The smile slipped just a smidgeon. He launched into his spiel. "I can work with any animal. I offer beginner and intermediate obedience classes, and I also offer private training if you're interested in competitive obedience."

"Oh, I don't know about competition," I said, "but I was at the dog show last weekend, and I'll admit, it got me curious." Wow, I was rocking this interview stuff. Only two minutes in, and I had managed to bring up the dog show.

He raised both eyebrows. "You were at the show?"

"Yes. It was… memorable."

He made a tight noise of agreement.

"It was unfortunate what happened to that lady. Mildred, I believe her name was." I tilted my head. "Did you know her?"

"Well enough. She was... not universally loved, but she knew her way around the show dog business."

I nodded, like that made perfect sense.

Nick chimed in. "It seems like a close-knit community. Must've shaken people up."

Billings looked briefly uncomfortable. Then he shrugged. "It did. But dog shows go on. That's how it is. One minute, someone's winning Best in Show, the next—well." He made a vague gesture with his hand. "There's always drama."

"Did you see anything suspicious that day?" I asked, careful to keep my tone light. "It just seemed like there were a lot of people milling around. Someone had to have seen something."

He hesitated. "If you're asking whether I saw someone tamper with her drink or slip something into her grooming bag, the answer is no."

"I wasn't," I lied. "But I'm curious why you brought up tampering with her drink."

His jaw tightened. "People talk. There were rumors."

"About?" Nick asked casually.

Billings glanced around as if the agility tunnels might be bugged. "Look. There's always tension. Jealousies. That woman made a lot of enemies. I'm not saying anyone wanted her dead, but if someone did, there'd be no end to the list of suspects." He studied me for a moment longer. "Hey, you're the vet, aren't you?"

I swallowed. "Yes."

"I heard the police were asking questions about *you*."

Of course, he had. How many other people knew?

Nick stepped forward slightly. "She's not under investigation. We're just trying to clear things up."

Billings gave him a look that said *uh-huh*. A wary expression replaced the friendly demeanor.

I pushed on. "I heard she owed you a lot of money."

"Excuse me?" His face flushed with an ugly shade of red that I had seen before—on Saturday, to be exact. "Frankly, I don't see what any of that has to do with your dog's behavior." He poked the air around my chest with a stubby finger. "And if you're in any way trying to suggest I had something to do with Mildred's death, consider the fact that I won't get a dime of the money she owes me now that she's dead."

Good point. I forced a smile. "You're right. I'm sorry. I certainly didn't mean to imply anything. It's just like you said, people talk."

His eyes narrowed. "Do you even have a dog you want trained, or is this just an excuse for you to come out here and point the finger at me?"

Nick rushed to my defense. "Goodness, no, Mr. Billings. Like Amy said, we never meant to imply anything."

Billings crossed his arms. "If you're not serious about training, I suggest you take your questions elsewhere."

"We'll be in touch," Nick said, steering me toward the car.

Billings' laser-beam glare followed us as we hustled back to the car and backed out of the driveway.

Once we'd escaped the house, I exhaled. "That went well."

"He's hiding something," Nick said. "I just don't know what." He chuckled. "But you did great for someone flying without a leash."

"I'm not so sure about that. I just made him mad. And suspicious. What if he hides out by the dumpster at my clinic and strangles me with a leash when I take out the trash?"

Nick shot me a look that said he found the scenario highly unlikely.

"Do you believe him?" I asked. "About not being involved?"

Nick's fingers drummed the steering wheel. "I believe he didn't like her. That part was honest. But he got awfully defensive when you brought up the money."

"Maybe he's tired of people bringing it up."

"Or maybe he's lying about something." Nick adjusted the rearview mirror.

I leaned back against the headrest. "So, what's your read?"

"I think he caught on pretty fast that we weren't there for obedience training. But he sure didn't want to talk about the murder. He wanted us gone."

We lapsed into silence. But it didn't seem awkward. I snuck glances at Nick's profile when I thought he wasn't looking.

Finally, I said, "What's our next move?"

He shot me a grin. "Want to buy a puppy?"

My brows drew together. "A puppy?"

"Yeah, I hear Joanna had a puppy sale that fell through."

I contemplated that suggestion. "I don't know. Pretending to scope out obedience training is one thing. Getting someone's hopes up for a sale you don't intend to go through with is another."

"We can pretend to be 'just looking.' When she mentions the price, which will be steep, we'll say it's more than we can afford."

"I don't know . . ."

"Look, we've got to figure out a way to talk to the other three people. I don't think Joanna's going to up and invite us over for tea and interrogation."

I swiveled to face him. "Martin Billings saw right through our ruse. What if Joanna does, too?"

"We'll be more subtle next time."

"I thought we were being subtle *this* time."

"We're learning as we go," said Nick.

I sighed. "All right. Do you know how to get in contact with her?"

"I can find her number." He cast me a sly look. "Are you okay with being my girlfriend?"

My heart did a somersault and banged into my ribs. Breathless, I said, "What?"

He chuckled. "My pretend girlfriend, I mean."

My ego deflated faster than a punctured balloon. "Oh, yeah, sure." Still, even pretending was better than nothing. Right?

We pulled up in front of my place. I unclipped my seatbelt but didn't move to open the door yet.

"You gonna be okay tonight?" he asked.

"Unless Billings sends a pack of bloodhounds after me, yeah."

Nick hesitated. "If he is hiding something, we'll find it. Just... stay alert, okay?"

"Thanks, Dad."

He gave me a look.

"I'll be fine," I added more seriously. "I've got two watchdogs—well, technically one and a half—and pepper spray."

Nick walked me to the door. "Call me if anything feels off."

I opened my door. "I will. And Nick, thanks for your help."

I watched as he headed back to the car and pulled away, his taillights disappearing into the dark. My stomach still fluttered from . . . something.

Both Sierra and Evie greeted me enthusiastically like I'd returned home from war. Evie had certainly come out of her shell in the last couple of days. I sat on the floor and gave them puppy loves.

"Girls, I have news. I have a pretend boyfriend."

Chapter Twelve

The phone rang as I was brushing my teeth for bed. "Hawo?" I mumbled around a mouthful of toothpaste. Foamy toothpaste dribbled down my chin, making me look like a rapid chipmunk.

"Are you still alive?"

Tess. I'd forgotten to call her. "Ho' on." I spit into the sink, rinsed, and wiped my mouth on a towel that probably wasn't clean. "I just got home," I lied.

"I was about five minutes away from calling the cops." Her scolding tone shifted from reprimand to nosiness. "So, how did it go? Is the dog trainer the killer?"

I flopped onto the bed with a groan. "I still don't know. He certainly didn't break down and make a dramatic confession like killers do on TV. In fact, he caught on to our subterfuge pretty quickly. But he did bring up a good point."

"Which was?"

"If he *had* killed Mrs. Blankenship, he'd be unlikely to ever recoup his ten grand. Not exactly a smart business move." I reminded her about the

Battleship's outstanding bill to Billings and the showdown between him and the dearly—and suspiciously—departed.

"Yeah, I suppose you're right. Suing her would be more profitable. Murder's bad for the bottom line."

"Exactly. Still, there's something fishy about him. I just don't know what it is yet." I ran my tongue over a glob of toothpaste that still clung to my lower right molar.

"What do you mean 'yet?' Don't tell me you're going to continue to poke around this guy?"

"I don't know." I propped a pillow against the headboard and cradled my arm behind my head. "He's rather creepy. Charming one minute, psycho the next, like someone flipping a light switch. He practically threw us off his property."

"Amy, you're really making me nervous. I wish you'd back off from all this amateur detective stuff. You're not Nancy Drew."

"Relax. We're leaving Mr. Billings alone for now."

"What does that mean? 'For now'?"

"Nick and I are going to visit Mrs. Papadopoulos tomorrow night."

"And which one is she again?"

"She's the breeder whose puppy sale fell through because of what Mrs. Blankenship told the prospective buyer."

"Oh yeah. To be honest, my money's on Billings. I mean, how homicidal can a puppy breeder be?"

I laughed. "You'd be surprised. You didn't see her breathing fire at the dog show."

"I don't suppose there's any talking you out of this death wish hobby you've developed?"

"Not as long as I'm the number one suspect. Besides, it's another chance to spend time with Nick."

"Ooooh." She dragged out the one syllable into three. "And how did *that* go?"

I sighed again. "He asked me to be his pretend girlfriend."

I could almost hear her eyebrows shoot up. "Pretend girlfriend? Is that, like, a thing?"

"Beats me. He told Billings I was his girlfriend as part of his cover story. Not that I'm complaining. With Nick, I'll take accidental affection over none."

"Be careful there, too. You don't need a broken heart *and* a life sentence."

"Thanks, Tess. You're such a ray of sunshine."

"I try. Now, hang up and go to bed. You have to attempt to be a normal vet tomorrow."

"No promises."

"Didn't think so. But don't say I didn't warn you."

I made it through the next day on autopilot, powered by adrenaline and an alarming amount of caffeine. Fortunately, the clinic blessed me with a light caseload—no emergencies, no swallowed tennis balls, and no irate pet parents who also happened to be litigation lawyers.

Tess, ever the voice of anxious reason, continued to try to talk me out of my impending rendezvous, but I stuck to my plan. An evening with Nick and puppies would be a great stress reliever.

Evie outran Sierra when they greeted me at the door, her short legs working double time. She placed her front feet halfway up to my knees, begging to be picked up. Her little tail waved hard enough to power a small fan as she bestowed doggy kisses on my cheek.

I was amazed by how quickly the tiny traitor had transferred her loyalty from the late Mrs. B to me. Then again, perhaps she viewed me as her savior. And, truth be known, I was becoming rather fond of the critter.

Surprisingly, Sierra did not appear to be jealous of Evie's shameless ploys to garner my attention. No growling, no passive-aggressive side eyes. If anything, she seemed delighted to have a pint-sized companion, even one who weighed less than her tail.

Still, I couldn't let myself get too attached. I figured I would have to give Evie up eventually. Surely Mrs. Blankenship had family somewhere who would want Evie, being the multi-winning champion show dog and all. Evie had to be worth a small fortune. But frankly, Evie seemed pretty content slumming it in pet-only status.

I fed the dogs and let them outside for a quick romp, then surveyed myself in the mirror—and immediately regretted it. The telltale signs of stress and lack of sleep made their presence known by the dark circles under my eyes. I quickly dabbed some concealer on the dark areas and hoped Nick wouldn't notice.

Nick arrived right on time, looking—if possible—even more annoyingly attractive than he had the night before. My stomach did a little happy dance, which my brain tried to quash with a stern *he relegated you to "pretend girlfriend." Remember?* But the twinkle in his gorgeous eyes didn't look like pretense.

"You look great," he said, which made my foolish heart skitter like a pre-teen with a crush.

"Maybe it's the absence of coffee stains on my shirt," I quipped.

He chuckled. "That, too. Would you like to grab a quick bite to eat before our mission?"

I shook my head. "I'm too nervous to eat. I'd probably choke on a breadstick."

"Okay, maybe after. Ready?" he inclined his head toward the car.

Deja vu hit as he opened the car door and helped me in. Not that I needed help, mind you, but I sure enjoyed the man fussing over me like this was an actual date. He even did that casual hand-on-my-back thing that made my spine go limp.

"I hope you have a plan," I said when he slid in behind the wheel. "I think I went off-script last night."

"Well, we are basically writing the script as we go." He grinned at me. "But I called Joanna—Mrs. Papadopoulos—and told her we were interested in seeing the puppy. That will get our feet in the door, so to speak."

Gratitude flowed over me for all Nick was doing for me. He didn't have to put himself out there like this, especially in something that could turn dangerous. He could have just given me the contact information and said, "Good luck, Jessica Fletcher."

"Nick, I want you to know how much I appreciate all your help. I know you don't have to be involved in any of this, and if you want to bow out, I'd totally understand." I twisted to face him, praying he wouldn't take me up on the offer.

He shot me a glance with that killer smile. Probably a poor choice of adjective. "Not a chance. I'm having too much fun."

I smiled back, full of way too much relief. "Okay, so what's the plan?"

"Like I said, we pretend to be interested in buying the puppy. And try to get her to talk about the dog show and Mrs. Blankenship. With any luck, she'll overshare something important."

I blew out a breath, my nerves fluttering. "I hope tonight goes smoother than last night. Martin Billings gives me the creeps."

Joanna Papadopoulos' house, located just a few blocks from the fairgrounds, was a picture of suburban perfection. Nestled in a quiet cul-de-sac, it had a tidy brick façade, glossy black shutters, and a wreath of silk magnolias on the front door. The lawn was neatly trimmed and edged with precision, and flower beds burst with color—azaleas, snapdragons, and pansies planted in careful rows. A bird feeder swayed gently from a shepherd's hook, and a cheerful garden flag with a cartoon Chihuahua and the words "Papa's Puppies" flapped in the gentle breeze.

Nick parked at the curb and gave a low whistle. "Somebody's got a landscaping service."

I scanned the property. "It's awfully nice. I wonder why Joanna was so upset over losing that sale. It doesn't look as though she's hurting for money."

He shrugged. "Maybe it was the slur to her reputation rather than the money."

He did make a valid point. Having your good name smeared stung, especially in the world of dog breeding, where gossip traveled faster than racing greyhounds.

The dogs announced our arrival before we raised the large brass knocker to rap on the door—sharp yaps from inside, muffled by the walls, high-pitched and persistent. Tiny dog alarms going off at full volume.

The ornate front door opened as we reached the porch. And that's where the suburban perfection ground to a screeching halt. The woman I'd seen at the fairgrounds stood in the foyer wearing purple stretch shorts and a red tank top, which showed an abundance of floppy upper arm skin. Her feet were bare with black painted toenails. Her grey hair stood up in a wild, frizzy mop in what could be described as "electrocuted poodle."

I almost wondered if she was an impostor who had ended up in the wrong house. Craning my neck beyond her, I spied an immaculate living area that smelled faintly of a collision between furniture polish and Bath and Body Works.

"You must be the ones interested in the puppy," she said with a broad smile. "I'm Joanna Papadopoulos. But, please, just call me Joanna. Come in, come in. The dogs are in the sunroom—I just let them in from the yard."

Once again, I had difficulty wrapping my mind around this gracious, if somewhat oddly dressed lady, and the irate woman who'd stomped into the dog show, her face contorted with rage, to confront Mildred Blankenship.

We walked through a pristine foyer into a large, airy room at the back of the house. How did someone with several dogs keep a house so spotless? Sunlight streamed through tall windows inside the sunroom, warming the tiled floor. A pack of Chihuahuas eyed us from a distance. Then one broke rank and made a beeline for Nick, sniffing his shoes and flopping onto her side for a belly rub.

"She's a flirt," the breeder said with a chuckle. "That's Lacey. She always picks the handsome ones."

Nick raised an eyebrow and crouched down, rubbing the dog's belly. "Good taste, I guess."

I knelt to greet the others, who approached with cautious optimism, wagging hesitant tails. I scratched a tan dog behind the ears.

"They're beautiful," I said. "So friendly, too."

"Thank you. I've worked hard on temperament," Joanna said proudly. "Health and personality are just as important as conformation, you know. I always say I raise companions first, show dogs second."

She moved to a low bench near the window and sat. One of the dogs jumped into her lap and curled up. "This one's Jasper. He's retired from the ring now but still thinks he's royalty."

"He looks like royalty," I said, smiling. "How many do you have?"

"Seven, currently. I've had as many as ten, but I've scaled back in the last few years. I'm getting too old to chase puppies all day."

I scanned the room—a shrine of doggy greatness with shelves lined with ribbons and plaques and photos of dogs standing in perfect poses with judges in suits. A few candid shots were tucked between the formal ones, showing dogs curled up on couches or wearing party hats at what looked like a birthday celebration.

"They live in the house with you?" I asked.

"Of course. They're family. In my opinion, people who keep their dogs in kennels out back shouldn't be breeding." Her smile tightened as though she were referring to someone in particular. "A dog raised in a cage isn't going to give you a good-natured pet. Or a good show dog, for that matter."

Joanna rose, placing Jasper on the floor, and retrieved a small glass jar off a shelf, handing it to me. Inside were homemade dog biscuits in the shape of bones, each one carefully stamped with what looked like tiny paw prints.

"Would you like to give them a treat?"

"Sure," I said. I crouched again as the dogs gathered eagerly. "Sit," I said, and they all immediately obeyed.

Somewhat surprised, I passed out biscuits. "They're very well-trained." These dogs had better manners than most of the folks at the DMV.

"They should be. They've all got their Canine Good Citizen titles. I run a tight ship around here." She gazed fondly at her animals, then said, "But you're here about the puppy."

"Yes. We'd love to see him. Or her," I said.

"Him. I'll be right back." She disappeared into another room and returned with a shiny black creature so tiny it would fit into my coat pocket.

She placed him in my lap, and my heart melted. Brown button eyes stared at me, and a little pink tongue flicked out to lick my hand, making me giggle.

"You're lucky. I had a buyer for him, but he backed out at the last minute."

What an opening! "Really?" I tried to sound nonchalant. "Why would anyone back out of buying this precious little cutie pie?"

A cloud crossed her face. "Well, to be perfectly honest, another breeder bad-mouthed me."

Nick pulled off a shocked expression that deserved an Oscar. "How terrible? Who would do such a thing?"

She pursed her lips, obviously trying to decide whether to take the high road or let loose with some well-deserved criticism of her nemesis. Finally, she said, "It really doesn't matter now. The individual passed away a few days ago. And one should only speak good of the dead."

From the struggle warring on her face, I could only imagine what she was thinking. *Mildred's dead. Good!*

I seized the wide-open opportunity. "Surely you aren't referring to the woman who died at the dog show on Saturday? Mrs. Blankenship?"

Joanna sighed. "Well, since you know about her unfortunate death, I suppose I may as well confirm that she was the one." Her eyes narrowed, and her gaze landed on something over my head. "After all I did for her, too. I mentored that woman. Got her started in the business. Then, when she began to do well, she repaid me by stabbing me in the back."

I clucked my tongue in true sympathy. I could well imagine Mrs. Blankenship biting the hand that fed her. So to speak. "I'm so sorry. What an ungrateful thing to do."

She returned her gaze to me and waved her hand as if brushing all the negativity away. Did all breeders have to master the dismissive wave?

"Oh, forgive me. I shouldn't have burdened you with all that nonsense. It's all water under the bridge now."

"Not at all," Nick piped up. "To be honest, we were at the dog show the other day and we observed her being quite nasty to several people."

Joanna nodded. "I'm not surprised." If she wondered whether or not she was one of the people we'd observed, she didn't let on.

I adopted a conspiratorial tone. "We heard she bribed the judge so her dog would win."

Joanna rolled her eyes. "Let me guess who you heard that nonsense from. Darlene McDougal."

"Yes," I replied, surprised she had nailed the source so fast.

Joanna tossed her head, setting her frizzy curls into motion like a windblown Brillo pad. "Darlene has been jealous of Mildred's success since the Reagan administration. "

I opened my mouth, but she was already winding up. For a woman who'd started out so closed-mouthed, she'd suddenly found her inner Chatty Cathy.

"The fact of the matter is, Darlene's dogs have never been as good as Mildred's. I should know. I taught Mildred how to breed quality dogs, and even if my protégé did turn on me like a rattlesnake, I can honestly say she would never stoop to bribing a judge."

"It's nice to know that Mrs. Blankenship had at least *some* integrity despite how many people she threw under the bus," I said.

"I don't know that integrity had anything to do with it. For one thing, judges take their jobs quite seriously. Bribery would get you kicked out of the competition so fast your leash would still be swinging in the ring. For another, Mildred won because she deserved to win. Period. Darlene's words are nothing but malicious gossip."

Nick and I remained quiet while Joanna seemed to ruminate on what she'd just revealed. I had to hand it to her. For someone who Mrs. Blankenship had steamrolled on her rise to the top, Joanna had no trouble giving credit where it was due—especially when it came to those top-tier show dogs.

After a moment, she leaned forward and whispered, as though any number of listening ears eavesdropped, "I heard she was poisoned."

"We heard that, too," said Nick, scooting closer. "Do you have any idea who might have done it?"

Joanna didn't flinch. Apparently, she did not consider the possibility that we might think her a suspect. Or she chose to ignore it. "No telling. She had a lot of enemies."

I pushed a bit harder. "I'll bet you were upset when she caused the sale of this darling puppy to fall through."

She sighed. "Oh, at the time, yes. She besmirched my character to the president of the kennel club, of all people, and I'll admit that really steamed me. It completely blindsided me, and I felt so betrayed that I said some things to Mildred that I now regret. I generally try to rise above these things." Her lips curled in a faint smile. "But I've never had any trouble selling my puppies." She rubbed her hands together. "Speaking of which, are you interested?"

"Oh, I absolutely love him," I replied truthfully. "How much are you asking?"

"My original contract was for two thousand dollars." She eyed me like a used-car salesman sensing weakness. "But I can tell you are a dog person. I'll let you have him for fifteen hundred."

I gulped. I still had student loans to repay. And my refrigerator was making death rattles. Plus, never in my life had I bought a dog. They always managed to find me.

"Oh, honey," said Nick. "I know you like him, but that's just a little steep for our budget."

Honey? I blinked, then remembered—fake girlfriend. Sighing dramatically, I said, "I shouldn't have gotten my hopes up. I knew buying a puppy from a good breeder would be more than we could afford." I rose to hand her back the puppy.

Nick got up and laid a hand on my arm. Very convincing. "I'm sorry, honey."

"Wait," said Joanna, refusing to take the puppy from my outstretched arms. "One thousand. My final offer. That's a steal."

"Oh, we understand you'd be taking a loss," said Nick, "but we can't—"

"Sold," I said.

Chapter Thirteen

"**Do you want** to tell me what you were thinking?" Nick asked as we drove away, the sweet pup asleep on my lap.

"Obviously, my heart overrode my head. But look at him, Nick. How could I resist?" I stroked the soft fur between his ears. "Besides, I got a good deal. She knocked one thousand dollars off the original asking price. That's like a clearance sale."

Nick snorted. "You do realize that the reason we were there was not to expand your menagerie. It was to investigate a murder." He rolled his beautiful eyes. "They say there's a sucker born every minute."

"Hey!" I pointed an indignant index finger at him. "I may be broke and impulsive, but I'm not a . . ." Yeah, I was a sucker. I might as well have had the word "sucker" tattooed on my forehead. I seriously didn't know where I was going to come up with the money I'd promised to send to Joanna, who had allowed me to take the puppy on my assurance that payment was forthcoming.

"Well, if nothing else, I don't think she killed

Mildred. She was up front with us without being defensive like Billings. She even had homemade dog biscuits, Nick, with paw prints stamped into them. That's not the behavior of a cold-blooded killer."

"She also wore purple biker shorts and had the hair of a mad scientist. Don't be too quick to let her off the hook. Remember how she practically spat nails when she entered the fairgrounds on Saturday? And her less-than-friendly confrontation with the Battleship?"

"True." I sighed.

"All that we really accomplished was acquiring you another dog. Which, I dare say, you don't need."

I gazed at the little ball of fur in my lap. "Oh, he doesn't even count as a whole dog. More like a 'doglet.' He won't eat much or take up much room."

Nick shook his head and chuckled. "You'll have to apply for a kennel license."

"What do you think of the name 'Corky'? He looks like a 'Corky,' don't you think?"

"I think you're going to wind up with your own reality show. Amy and Corky solve a murder."

I grinned. "Only if you make guest appearances." Nick's idea actually had merit. With my own reality series, I could make a bundle of money and pay off my debt for Corky, as well as my student loans.

The corner of Nick's mouth twitched. "After what happened tonight, though, I'm a bit reluctant to use the same ploy with Darlene McDougal."

"True. I don't think we can use that puppy-buying excuse again unless I sell a kidney. And I'm very attached to both of them. Besides, we don't know if she has any puppies for sale."

Nick exhaled slowly. "We'll have to come up with

a different strategy. Something low-cost." He glanced over at Corky. "You know, if you end up going to prison, I'm not taking that mutt."

"You say that now. But just look at those eyes." As if on cue, Corky stirred and directed his big brown eyes to Nick.

"Swell. I guess you're not the only sucker in the car."

Obviously. But I was the one who was going to be thrown into debtors' prison along with a federal penitentiary. "But what excuse are we going to give to question Darlene?"

"I don't know. I'll have to think about it."

Nick insisted on stopping for dinner since he was starving. I wrapped Corky in the baby blanket Joanna had sent with me and tucked him into my oversized purse as we walked into Denny's. We smiled at the hostess like everything was perfectly normal, and I didn't carry contraband, with my bag shifting ever so slightly.

As she led us to a table, I whispered, "He's asleep. If you do anything to wake him up, I'm stuffing *you* in the bag." It wasn't that I hadn't wanted more time with Nick, but he had his heart set on a Denny's Grand Slam breakfast, and the presence of Corky complicated matters a bit.

"I think you'll need a bigger bag," he said out of the corner of his mouth.

We slid into the red vinyl seats, and I perused the

menu alone since Nick already knew what he wanted. My stomach had finally stopped clenching when we left Joanna's house with Corky, and it now reminded me I hadn't attended to it since lunch, which was several hours ago.

Nick leaned across the Formica table. "Tell me again why we couldn't leave him in the car."

"Nick, he's a baby. You don't leave babies alone in cars." I took a peek in my bag, relieved to see Corky sound asleep.

The waitress approached carrying two glasses of water and silverware. Nick placed his order while I hurried to decide what I wanted. The less time the woman hovered over our table, the better. But she seemed in no rush. Perhaps it had something to do with the flirty glances she kept throwing Nick's way. She barely made eye contact with me when I told her I wanted scrambled eggs and toast.

She finally finished taking our order just as a muffled whine came from my purse. Her brows drew together in confusion. "Did that noise just come from your bag?"

My mind went blank. Then I heard myself blurt out, "Oh, I must have left my phone on vibrate. It has a new tone."

Nick choked on his water. I frantically reached into my bag and rubbed my "phone's" head.

The waitress nodded slowly, then turned and walked away to put in our order.

Nick coughed into his napkin and said, "Nice save. You're a good liar."

I didn't know whether to take that as a compliment or not. "Nick," I whispered, "what if he won't be quiet?"

"Then we'll have an 'emergency' and ask her to pack our food to go."

I let out a slow breath and kept rubbing Corky's head, pretending I wasn't cradling a tiny fugitive in my purse. My eyes flicked to the waitress—still across the room—thank goodness. The place was nearly empty this late, except for a couple seated directly behind me, close enough to overhear our drink order and any suspicious yips.

Great. Of all the nights to dine in a half-dead restaurant, we picked the one where a single puppy sneeze could echo like a fire alarm. I silently wished for a crowd. A little background noise. A table full of bachelorette giggles or a family of loud chewers. Anything to drown out the sounds of a smuggled canine.

A few minutes later, the waitress returned bearing food, lingering to ask Nick, not me, if everything looked okay and if he needed anything else. And, of course, Corky chose that moment to whine again.

She turned, her expression one of disbelief. "That is the weirdest vibrate tone I have ever heard."

"Yes, it is," I agreed with a laugh. "It's new. But it kind of grows on you." I gave her a pointed stare. "I probably should answer that. It might be important."

She seemed to take the hint and left, while I pretended to pull my cell phone from my purse and said, "Let me call you back" into empty air.

Fortunately, Corky settled down, and we made it through most of the meal. But just when I accepted Nick's offer of a strip of bacon, a tiny head popped up, followed by two little legs scrambling for purchase on the top of my purse.

"He's making a break for it!" hissed Nick.

I pinched a piece of egg and held it to Corky's mouth. "I guess the smell of bacon was too irresistible." The pup eagerly devoured the egg. "He must be hungry." I knew tiny-breed puppies like Chihuahuas had to eat frequently to keep their blood sugar from getting too low. I continued to finger-feed him bits of egg.

The woman at the next table craned her neck. "What is that? Do they have a *dog* in a restaurant? Doesn't the Board of Health have rules against dogs in restaurants?"

"Don't say anything," the man said under his breath. "If it's an emotional support animal, you can get in trouble for questioning people with disabilities."

I tried to stuff Corky down in my purse, but he refused to go in. He was mighty determined for such a small creature. I finally laid him in my lap and covered him with my napkin as I continued to sneak bites of egg to him.

The waitress came back with the check and did a double-take at my napkin. Too late, I realized a tiny tail poked out.

"It belongs to him," I said, blaming everything on Nick. I figured the waitress wouldn't report *him* to management.

Nick winked at her and shot her his megawatt smile. "Guilty. We couldn't leave him in the car."

Her eyes darted between us before returning to Nick. "You know what? I'm going to pretend like I didn't see anything. Have a good night." She moved to the next table.

I noticed she'd written her phone number on the back of the check. I grabbed it and said, "My treat. For all your help."

"You'd better leave a big tip," he muttered.

As Nick drove me home, I reflected again on how much I appreciated his help. Surely any man so willing to involve himself in my issues had to feel *some* interest in me. Unless he was the killer and determined to keep an eye on me.

The next day, I had a full slate of farm calls, which was perfect—sunshine, wide-open spaces, the chance to clear my head, and no overly curious technician breathing down my neck. A win-win.

Unfortunately, Tess ambushed me before I could even toss my purse onto my desk, which was good since it contained one very squirmy Chihuahua.

"Tell me everything." She leaned against the door she had closed when she followed me into the office.

"Good morning to you, too."

"Yeah, yeah, whatever. You didn't call. You didn't text. I've had to imagine the details, and you know how dangerous that is."

"I got home late again." This time, I told the truth, with a sappy smile plastered on my face.

Corky's head popped out of my purse like a jack-in-the-box, startling Tess and causing her to emit a high-pitched squeal like a frightened pig.

"What in the world?" She clutched her heart like an actress in a bad movie.

"I was going to tell you about him, but you

waylaid me before I had a chance." I pulled Corky out and offered him to her. "This is Corky."

"Oh! Isn't he the most adorable . . ." Her voice instantly pitched into that high, squeaky register reserved for babies, puppies, and occasionally cupcakes. She got lost in Corky Land, baby-talking him and showering kisses on his little round head.

"I had to bring him to work with me. He's too little to leave by himself." I went on to fill her in on our adventures from the evening before, but I'm not sure she was listening to me. I yawned. "I got precious little sleep last night. He cried. I cried. For such a little guy, he sure can demand a lot of attention."

Sierra had sniffed him and looked him over before giving me a cocked-head expression that said, *Seriously? When are you going to stop bringing these things home?*

Evie had mostly ignored him.

Corky had peed on the living room carpet the minute I set him down. I groaned. It had been a long time since I'd had to housebreak a puppy. I'd forgotten how time-consuming that whole process was. At least he had a tiny bladder.

"But, Amy," Tess said, still nuzzling Corky, "I don't understand. How does buying a puppy you can't afford help you to solve a murder?"

I sighed. "Good question. It doesn't. Probably. But I don't think Joanna did it. She's too . . . I don't know. Nice." Except for when she verbally gutted Mildred Blankenship like a trout.

Tess continued to coo over Corky. "I might just steal you from your mama."

"For a thousand bucks, he's yours," I said.

She stopped mid-coo. "A thousand dollars? Holy cow! Did he come with a trust fund?"

"He was a bargain," I said defensively. "Trudy of the no-last-name paid Mrs. Blankenship three thousand dollars for a puppy that developed epilepsy."

"Well, it just goes to show some people have more money than sense."

I hoped Tess referred to Trudy and not me. Because I had neither money *nor* sense.

"Anyway," I said, stretching, "you've got Corky duty this morning. I've got cows to poke and horses to harass."

"It'll be tough, but someone has to do it." Tess slipped him into her pocket and left the office.

Chapter Fourteen

Outside, my large animal technician, Joyce, was loading supplies into my truck when I emerged from the office. I'd hired Joyce for my large animal calls once or twice a week because Tess informed me from the get-go that she wasn't going near any animal that could end her career with one well-placed kick. I liked Joyce. She was efficient, organized, and better yet, quiet.

Except for today. "Did you hear about that awful murder at the dog show on Saturday?" she said, the moment I started the engine. Small town. News traveled fast. I only hoped the news of my involvement hadn't crept up the local grapevine as well.

"Yes, I did." I refused to elaborate further. Joyce didn't know I had been there, and I didn't particularly want to enlighten her. I hoped my not picking up the thread of the conversation would end it. No such luck.

"They say the woman was poisoned."

I gave her a noncommittal "hmm" and reached for my sunglasses, like they might shield me from talking about the murder. "Who's our first call?"

"Huh?" Joyce blinked at me, clearly not ready to let go of the juicy murder gossip. But she recovered quickly. "Oh. We're pulling Coggins tests on several horses at the Treadway Stables."

The Treadways were my kind of people—calm, competent, and most importantly, not there during most appointments. Nothing against horse folks, but they often attracted other horse folks who were "experts" or saw something on TikTok. These people didn't need the inconvenience or expense of obtaining a veterinary degree, as they already knew everything there was to know about equine medicine, which always made me wonder why they needed my services.

With any luck, today would be drama-free. But the way my luck had gone all week . . .

We pulled into the Treadway Stables, and Joyce hopped out to open the gate. As I drove through, my stomach dropped at the sight of a familiar SUV parked by the barn.

No. Not today. What was she doing here? I almost did a U-turn and headed on to our next appointment.

Too late. Carla Pangborn (I secretly called her Painborn), my most high-maintenance horse client, emerged from the barn waving her hot-pink manicured hands.

"Dr. Dixon! I'm so glad to see you. I have a teeny-tiny problem with my new show pony, Louie."

I plastered on a smile. "I thought you boarded your horses at Magnolias."

"I did," she said with a dramatic eye roll, "but I moved them here. Magnolias has simply gone downhill. Sub-par, in my opinion."

Not to mention the fact that Treadway Stables

charged less.

"Louie seems to be a bit *off,*" she continued. "Not lame, exactly, but not quite right in his left rear leg. I read about this rare neurological condition online but can't remember what they called it. Maybe you know."

I glanced helplessly at Joyce. "Gee, I'm sorry, Mrs. Pangborn"—I worked hard not to slip and call her "Painborn"—"but we're on a tight schedule today. Perhaps we can set up—"

"Oh, it will only take a minute," she insisted, latching onto my arm and towing me toward the barn.

Joyce shrugged, not doing anything to come to my rescue.

I sighed. Since I was here, I might as well have a quick look at the pony. Not having to come back out a second time to deal with Carla seemed like a good idea. She tugged me into the barn and out the other side into a sunny paddock, where a handsome Shetland pony stood nibbling grass.

"Hi, there, fella," I said, approaching slowly and holding out my hand.

Louie pinned back his ears and moved to the farthest corner of the paddock, eyes narrowed.

"He doesn't like strangers," said Carla. "But he loves sugar cubes." She reached into her pocket and extracted several of the treats, plunking them into my hand.

"Perhaps it would be better if you offered him the treats," I suggested. "Then you can grab his halter and hold him for me."

"Oh, he won't let me handle him," she said, as though I were daft.

"Then how do you . . ." *show him?* Never mind. I

shook my head and handed Joyce half the sugar cubes. "You go one way and I'll go the other."

She nodded and started moving in on the pony from the left while I went right. Louie's nostrils flared like a bull in a cartoon, and he bolted right between us. I lunged and missed, landing flat on the ground with a frustrated grunt.

"Oh, Louie, you naughty boy," called Carla from where she stood safely and comfortably in the shade of the barn. "He's just playing hard to get."

I pinched my lips. I could wrangle the most obstinate large animals. Including a terrifying emu named Gary. No pint-sized horse was going to beat me.

I got to my feet and brushed off my coveralls, determination set in my jaw. Louie stood out of reach, blowing loudly through his nose like a tiny fire-breathing dragon.

"Try it again," I told Joyce. "Channel your inner pony whisperer."

She took a cautious step forward, extending a hand with the sugar cubes. Louie shot forward and snatched the sugar clean out of her palm, then galloped off, bucking joyfully, clearly enjoying this game.

Joyce stared at her drool-covered hand. "Maybe my inner pony whisperer needs to be a bit louder."

"I'm going to start charging by the hour," I muttered, watching our schedule disintegrate.

We continued to chase the beast around the paddock for the next thirty minutes with no success. At least I got my cardio in for today. I leaned against the fence, out of breath and out of patience. Joyce doubled over beside me, her hands on her knees, sweat plastering her bangs to her forehead.

Louie trotted past us, a smug expression on his horsey face.

"He's not even tired," panted Joyce.

"I am," I said. "I'm dying. I think I've lost five pounds." I hated to throw in the towel, but we'd been playing cat and mouse for thirty minutes. I knew when to call it quits. I had just been outwitted by a Shetland with a Barbie mane.

I turned to Mrs. Painborn, who had somehow acquired a latte during our rodeo. "I'm sorry, but unless you can get him back into his stall, we can't—"

"Oh, of course." She disappeared into the barn and came back with a feed bucket. "Louie, darling, time to come in." She rattled the bucket, and Louie's head popped up like a meerkat. Then he trotted after her into the barn and straight into his stall like she was the Pied Piper and he was a rat. Fitting analogy.

Joyce and I exchanged a look of pure disbelief.

I gritted my teeth. Why hadn't the obtuse woman thought to do this earlier? In the stall's narrow space, Joyce and I converged on Louie. She managed to grab his halter and hang on, despite his attempt to tear her arm out of the socket by jerking his head. I yanked the bucket from Carla and set it on the ground in front of him. His muzzle disappeared into the pail.

With my heart still racing, I crouched to examine his left rear leg, slowly lifting the hoof, and nearly lost my front teeth when he kicked his leg back like a ninja.

"Oh, he doesn't usually do that," said Carla, as I contemplated the concussion I had narrowly escaped.

"That's reassuring," I muttered. "Drastic times call for drastic sedation. I think he has a sole abscess."

"Sedate him? Oh, I don't know about that." The

blood drained from Carla's spray-tanned face. "Are you sure it's an abscess? Maybe it's Lyme disease. Or West Nile."

I took a deep breath through my nose and silently counted to ten. "It's not Lyme or West Nile. It's a sole abscess. That means there's a pocket of pus in his hoof, and it hurts. The sedation will keep him from feeling the pain." *And kicking me into the next county.*

She wrung her hot-pink manicured hands. "Oh dear. That sounds expensive."

You have no idea, lady, who's holding a ten-dollar latte and wearing designer boots. "I'm afraid we have no choice." Without another word, I marched back to the truck and returned with my large animal box.

After sedating Louie, the job went quickly. We left the groggy gremlin with Mrs. Painborn, pulled our blood work on the *scheduled* horses, and rushed to our next call—two hours late, drenched in sweat, and with our morale in the septic tank.

"I'm seriously thinking about giving up large animal work," I said to Joyce, as I barreled down the road. "Devoting my entire career to sock-eating Labradors is becoming more and more attractive."

"At least it doesn't hurt as much when they kick you in the head."

Chapter Fifteen

The only good thing about today was that I was so busy I didn't have time to dwell on uplifting topics like murder, life sentences, and the fashion appeal of orange jumpsuits. Between playing catch-up on my workload and skipping lunch, I was running on fumes—and still behind. All thanks to Mrs. Painborn and Louie.

Okay. Fine. There were a few good things about today. Corky's sweet puppy breath for one. And the warm, tail-wagging greetings from Sierra and Evie when I stumbled into the house, face-planted on the sofa, and groaned like a deflated accordion. I debated whether I could muster the energy to crawl into the kitchen and nuke a microwave dinner. Then, like a miraculous beacon of hope, my phone rang. Nick! My dead body sprang back to life.

"Hey," he greeted, his voice perking me up like jumper cables on a dead battery. "I'm afraid I don't have a plan for getting us in to see Darlene McDougal tonight."

"It's okay. I'm so whipped tonight, I probably

can't lie convincingly anyway." My brain and body had officially clocked out somewhere between the Weimaraner who'd stuck his tongue in the paper shredder and the Beagle who, much to his surprise, had actually *caught* a squirrel. The squirrel had put up a valiant fight, inflicting several deep bite wounds before disappearing into the treetops.

"Have you had dinner yet?" Nick asked.

Suddenly, I got a second wind. Like a typhoon. "No."

"How about if I bring over some Chinese food and we can brainstorm our next move?"

"Great, I didn't get lunch, so I'm starved." Panic followed as I glanced down at myself. *Great!* I looked like something the cat dragged in. Or, more likely, something the cat wouldn't bother to drag in. "Thirty minutes?" Time for a quick shower to wash off the horse smell.

The shower and the thought of Nick—and food— perked me up. He arrived a half-hour later, and although my damp hair still had a mind of its own, it didn't smell like a barnyard. I ushered him in to my small kitchen, where he deposited a massive shopping bag full of take-out containers, spreading them across the table like he was unveiling a royal feast.

"Gee, I said I was hungry, but I don't think I can eat all this." I eyed all the little white boxes spread out on the table. In truth, I was hungry enough to eat a horse—Louie came to mind—but I didn't want Nick to think I *ate* like a horse.

Nick shrugged. "I didn't know what you liked, so I got a variety."

"I'll say." I grinned at him. "Thanks. This is

wonderful." I pulled out two plates and silverware and grabbed two water bottles from the refrigerator.

He bowed his head and said a quick prayer, then we dug in. For several blissful minutes, my mouth was too preoccupied to speak. Despite my initial resolve to eat like a civilized woman, my hunger won. I tore through the food like a starving raccoon raiding a trash can in the moonlight, devouring the meal with reckless abandon. If Nick thought less of my unladylike manners, he was polite enough not to mention it. Oh well, pretend girlfriends don't have to impress anyone, right?

Finally, I came up for air. And an idea.

"I remember Trudy of the no-last-name laying into Mrs. Blankenship because she'd bought a puppy from her that she wanted to breed and show that developed epilepsy. What if we take Corky to Darlene McDougal and tell her we're interested in breeding him with one of her dogs?" I glanced at the tiny love muffin curled up in Sierra's bed next to Evie. Doglets had completely usurped my poor girl's bed. "Obviously not right away."

Nick nodded. "That's a good idea. We can pretend to solicit her advice, and if and when the breeding question comes up down the road, we can say we've changed our minds. Plus, you won't be coming home with another dog."

I chuckled. "I wonder what Joanna would say about being in-laws with Darlene?"

He smiled. "I got the distinct impression the two aren't exactly BFFs."

"Except they both disliked Mildred Blankenship. You know what they say. The enemy of my enemy—"

"Might be a murderer," Nick finished grimly, the smile fading.

I sighed. "You know, for all our efforts at trying to figure out who the killer is, we've not gotten very far."

"Patience, Amy. We're just getting started." He rose and began depositing empty cartons in the trash can.

I followed, placing the dishes in the sink. "But what if the killer isn't one of our four suspects? For all we know, the Battleship could have had run-ins with a dozen other people on Saturday whom we didn't observe. Or it could have been someone who didn't fight with her that day but who held a long-standing grudge against her and decided to take action."

He stopped and placed his hands on my shoulders, which made my knees turn to jelly. "I think you're over-reaching. My bet is on one of the four. They all had motive and opportunity."

How I wanted to lean in and lay my head on his chest. But I reminded myself once again of my pretend girlfriend status. "I wish this whole investigation were over. I don't like living with the threat of a prison sentence hanging over my head."

"Be glad they don't still hang convicted murderers." Nick's eyes danced with merriment.

"Gee, that makes me feel so much better."

"How about we watch some mindless television and decompress?"

I found the idea of curling up with Nick on my sofa to watch television rather appealing. Okay, I found it *very* appealing. "Anything but *Murder She Wrote*."

Two hours later, I woke myself with an unladylike snort to see credits rolling over a dramatic orchestral swell. I rubbed my bleary eyes and focused on the screen, totally clueless as to what movie I had *not* just watched. Nick still sat beside me, a smirk tugging at his mouth. My dignity disappeared somewhere under the couch with the remote.

Inwardly groaning, I said, "How long was I asleep?" My cheeks burned with humiliation.

"You nodded off about the time 'Paramount Presents' came up on the screen."

Scrubbing a hand over my face to clear the sleep-fog, if not the embarrassment, I said, "Why didn't you wake me?" I hoped I hadn't drooled on myself. A quick swipe across my dry chin relieved that fear, though my neck felt like it had been twisted into a pretzel.

He shrugged. "You said you'd had a tough day. I figured you needed your sleep."

"Yeah, but . . . I'm sorry, Nick. I didn't mean to be such lousy company."

"No problem. I should have just left and let you sleep, but I got interested in the movie." He rose and stretched, sending electrical sparks into every nerve cell of my body. "You'll have to rewatch it later. I'll see you tomorrow for our interrogation of Mrs. McDougal. Assuming I can get a hold of her."

I smiled. "Thank you. For everything."

He bent and brushed his lips against my forehead. "Good night, Amy. Get some rest."

And then he was gone.

Too stunned to react, I simply watched as he walked out the door. My forehead tingled from his kiss. Did this possibly mean my status as pretend girlfriend had changed? Now I knew I wouldn't sleep all night.

I floated into work the next day on a cloud of ecstasy and caffeine. Of course, Tess of the eagle-eye noticed the difference in me immediately.

"I want details," she said, tailing me like a bloodhound into the office.

Pulling Corky from my purse, I replied, "I slept with Nick last night."

Tess gasped so hard that I feared she might swallow her tongue. "Amy! You don't even kiss on the first date!"

My hands flew to my face. "Oh my gosh! No, I mean . . . That came out all wrong." I tried to undo the damage by explaining what had really happened, but my tongue kept tripping over itself. I ended the twisted diatribe by saying, "And then he kissed me."

A wicked grin lit up her face.

"On the forehead," I quickly clarified before she began planning my bridal shower. "Do you think that means something?"

She gave me a slow, mischievous grin. "I would say it means you need to aim a little lower."

The very image made my insides go squishy. "Honestly, Tess, I can't cope with all of this right now. Trying to catch a murderer and falling for a guy I just met is too overwhelming."

She parked her derriere on the edge of my desk and took Corky from me. "Sometimes life takes unexpected turns. What's your next move?"

I told her about our excuse to question Darlene McDougal. "But I still have no idea how to track down the last suspect, Trudy."

"Maybe Mrs. McDougal knows her."

"Good thought. I'll try to remember to bring Trudy up tonight."

"Meanwhile, back to reality. You've got vet work to do. I've got the surgery set up for your first case."

"What is it?"

"An ear hematoma on a German shepherd. A big one."

"German shepherd or hematoma?"

"Both."

I made a face. Ear hematomas tended to be way down on the list of my favorite surgeries. But the bloody mess would keep my mind occupied. I needed a distraction to keep my mind off Nick and murderers. Mostly Nick.

Chapter Sixteen

Nick and I spent a solid ten minutes debating whether or not Corky should tag along to our meeting with Darlene McDougal, but in the end, he came along.

"She might want to see the future baby daddy of her precious show dogs," I argued. "And who could resist this face?" I held Corky up like Simba from *The Lion King*. "Plus, an adorable puppy might loosen her tongue."

"And keep us out of Denny's," muttered Nick.

Darlene McDougal met us at the door wearing the same expression she'd had at the dog show—like someone had just tracked mud on her antique rug.

"Thank you so much for seeing us," I gushed, dialing up the charm. "I appreciate your expertise and guidance." I smiled at Nick. "As my boyfriend mentioned, I'm new to all of this, and to have a breeder of your reputation willing to advise me . . . Well, I'm thrilled."

Darlene regarded us like something offensive she'd accidentally stepped in. Her close-cropped, fire-engine shade of red hair and icy blue eyes made her appear as warm as a Minnesota winter. Long, fake, neon green nails sprouted from the ends of her fingers, reminding me of the Wicked Witch of the West.

Through pinched lips, she said, "As I told the young man, I'm not sure how I can help you. I'm not interested in breeding my champion dogs with novices' pets." She blew out a sigh. "But since you're here, come in and sit down. I'll do what I can."

She led us into a modest living room that smelled like someone had tried to drown dog pee with Febreze. Nick and I took seats on the sagging sofa, which wheezed under our weight when we sat down.

Darlene parked on the matching armchair across from us, her legs crossed and arms folded across her chest.

She's going to be one tough nut to crack. "Let me show you my new puppy," I said brightly, producing Corky from my purse like a magician with a rabbit. Surely, he could melt the most frigid heart.

Darlene's sour expression remained firmly in place. "Where did you get him?"

"From Joanna Papadopoulos," I said with pride.

Darlene snorted. "Well, that's your first mistake."

I turned wounded eyes to Nick. Her words crushed me, even if my hopes of mixing Corky's genes with Darlene's dogs' DNA were merely a ploy.

"Why? What do you mean?" asked Nick.

"The woman is a has-been, second-rate, washed-up breeder."

Funny. That's what she said about you. I managed to keep from saying the words aloud.

"Oh?" I crinkled my forehead with what I hoped came across as concern rather than disgust at the woman's mean words.

"Yes. I wish you'd come to me first. I could have sold you a quality puppy."

Not happening. Can't afford another puppy.

She turned her piercing gaze on Corky, who blinked innocently. Her nose wrinkled in distaste. "I'm afraid that dog is not show or breeding material."

My heart sank for no good reason. Although I had no intention of breeding Corky, to be told these hurtful things was like calling my baby ugly, which, I guess, technically, she was.

"What's wrong with him?" I asked defensively, clutching Corky to my chest as though that would protect him from the woman's insults.

"The question is, what's *not* wrong with him? His head is too flat, his forehead is undefined, his eyes are too deeply set, his ears are too small, and his tail is too straight."

Yikes! I thought he was perfect! Disappointment oozed from my pores.

She stood, clearly done with our visit. "I'm sorry you wasted your time and money—"

"Wait!" I cried, flailing for a lifeline as our one chance at interrogation walked toward the door.

Darlene stopped, mid-step. "What?"

What indeed? I shot a helpless look at Nick.

"Uh," he stuttered. "Perhaps you can show us your dogs so we can see what to look for. In case we, uh, want to get another puppy."

Brilliant idea! Not only was Nick easy on the eyes, but he was clever. He was clearly wasting his time as an insurance adjuster. He was pure improv material.

She seemed to ponder Nick's request while I held

my breath.

"All right," she said finally, a hint of reluctance in her voice. "But I'm not in the habit of selling puppies to amateurs."

"That's okay. We realize we're in way over our heads." I gave her a self-deprecating smile that I hoped didn't look more like a creepy grimace. I was still miffed from her less-than-complimentary comments about my baby.

"Come with me." She led us through the house to an enclosed patio, where wall-to-wall Chihuahuas occupying large crates greeted us with high-pitched yaps. It looked like a Chihuahua maximum security prison. The odor nearly made me gag, and in my line of business, it takes a pretty foul odor to spoil my appetite.

I frowned at Nick. Joanna had specifically denounced this type of dog handling. He gave me a tight-lipped nod, clearly as revulsed as I by the doggy prison. *Prison!* The irony struck me like a bolt of lightning. I stared at my own fate unless we could solve this murder.

Darlene opened a crate and withdrew a shivering dog I recognized as Clementine. "Quiet!" she bellowed, and the chorus of yapping died like she'd turned off a faucet.

She held Clementine like a trophy, which I suppose she was, even though she was a second-place trophy. "Now, you see how this dog has a rounded skull."

"Oh, yes," I said, reaching over to palpate the domed noggin.

Darlene jerked the dog from under my fingers like I carried deadly germs.

"She doesn't like to be touched by strangers." The reprimand took me aback. Didn't Clementine have to undergo pawing, so to speak, by strange judges in the show ring?

"Sorry," I muttered.

"And you see her prominent forehead? There's a pronounced angle where the forehead meets the muzzle."

"Ah, yes," I admitted, although the word "hydrocephalus" sprang to mind.

"And her eyes are large and impressive."

Bug-eyed.

Darlene ran Clementine's ears through her fingers. "And see how large and erect her ears are?"

Bat radar.

She droned on about Clementine's body proportions while I tuned her out—until I spotted a familiar-looking long-haired Chihuahua in another crate. My heart did a somersault. "Wait!" I blurted once again, cutting her off in mid-sentence.

Darlene's mouth clamped shut, and her eyes grew large as if I'd slapped her with a raw fish.

"I'm so sorry to interrupt you, but that dog over there"—I pointed—"isn't that Mildred Blankenship's dog?"

She stiffened. "Yes, how do you know?"

Okay, time to 'fess up. But only to a point.

"Well, you see, I was the veterinarian on duty at the county dog show last Saturday, and I recognize that dog." The one who got away. The one that Nick and I had spent a long time searching for. I forced a laugh. "Although why I remember that particular dog, I couldn't tell you. I saw so many dogs that day. Must be

because he's so handsome. He's got a gorgeous coat."
Stop babbling.

Darlene clearly smelled trouble. Her expression turned wary, and her voice took on a self-justifying tone. "If you were at the dog show, then you know about Mildred's horrible death. Someone had to take in her dogs."

Or steal.

"How very kind of you to do so," Nick said, oozing with sincerity.

She narrowed her gaze, apparently trying to decide whether or not to believe him.

"Yes. Poor things," I added. "Does she not have any family to take them?" I tried to sound innocent and concerned.

"None who would want them." Darlene placed Clementine back in her crate. She seemed to realize the conversation had shifted from show dog perfection to the acquisition of the deceased's property. "Except I couldn't find her last dog, Evangelina Rose. I'm terribly worried about what happened to her." Her voice dripped with anxiety.

"Oh, I've got her," I piped up, realizing my mistake too late. I wanted to hit "rewind."

Her eyes locked on mine with sniper precision. "And *how*, may I ask, did *you* end up with her?"

"We found her huddled behind a crate after everyone had left," Nick said. "All alone. We didn't know what to do with her, and we couldn't just leave her there, so Amy took her home."

Those laser-sharp eyes burned into me. "Well, I'm relieved to hear she's all right." She stepped closer, invading my personal bubble. "You can bring her to me. I'll take care of her."

My mouth went dry, and my brain scurried like a hamster on a wheel to come up with a reason not to turn Evie over to this horrible woman.

"Oh, Mrs. McDougal," said Nick, "clearly you have your hands full with taking in Mrs. Blankenship's dogs in addition to your own."

"Yes," I croaked out. "Evie's no bother, really."

"Evie?" Second mistake. Darlene regarded me as though I'd uttered a blasphemy. "It's completely out of the question for you to keep her. Evangelina Rose is a champion show dog. You have no business with a dog like that."

My hackles rose. "With all due respect, Mrs. McDougal, I *am* a licensed veterinarian. I'm not exactly an amateur in the dog-care department."

Her lips disappeared. "I'm fully aware of the capabilities of veterinarians," she said, making my profession sound equivalent to "people who clip guinea pig nails for a living."

"However, you yourself admitted you don't have the training or the expertise to manage the unique requirements of a champion show dog." She pointed a judgmental finger at Corky. "Just look at the train wreck you purchased."

I felt my chin begin to wobble, and tears stung my eyes. If we didn't get out of here soon, I *might* just commit a murder.

"Thank you for your time," Nick said, laying a hand on my elbow and steering me toward the front door. "We'll be in touch." He hustled me down the hall.

"I *want* that dog!" Darlene barked, nipping at our heels.

Nick flung open the front door and shoved me through it. "We'll think about it and let you know," he called over his shoulder.

"You haven't heard the end of this. I will take you to court! I *will* get that dog!" she shrieked as we jumped into the car.

Nick burned rubber getting away like we'd just robbed a bank, while I dissolved in tears.

"Nick," I blubbered. "Can she legally take Evie away from me?"

"I doubt it," he said, reaching over to squeeze my hand. "She'd have to prove ownership, and last I checked, bellowing like a toddler in meltdown mode isn't admissible in court."

"I can't afford another lawyer." My crying morphed into ugly sobs. "Why did I open my big mouth and tell her I had Evie?"

"Because you're a good person," he said, with gentle calmness. "You didn't want her to worry about Evie. How were you to know she'd turn into Cruella De Vil?"

"We didn't even get to question her about the murder." I hiccupped. "All we did was stir up more trouble."

Nick's jaw clenched. "She's evil. I wouldn't be surprised if she didn't murder the Battleship to steal her dogs."

I sat up straighter, the fog of emotion parting just enough to let in the lightbulb moment. I sucked in a calming breath. "Oh my gosh! You're right. She had the perfect motive. Jealousy and greedy ambition."

"With Mildred out of the way, Darlene takes over her show dogs and goes on to win championship after championship. She gets the dogs, the titles, and the glory."

My blood turned to ice. I knew, without a shadow of a doubt, that we'd provoked a potential killer. One who'd do anything to get her hands on Evie—including murdering *me*.

Chapter Seventeen

"It's Darlene McDougal, I'm sure of it," I said to Tess before she had a chance to waylay me the next morning.

Her eyes grew big. "Why, what happened?"

I jerked my head toward the office. When we were alone behind the closed door, I whispered, "She took Mrs. B's dogs. Now nothing will stand in her way of winning."

"What do you mean she took Mrs. B's dogs? Did she dognap them?" Tess cried.

"Shh, keep your voice down." I waved my hand like a breeder pro. "Since the woman's dead, someone had to take care of her dogs. And Darlene saw it as her civic duty to take on the responsibility." I made air quotes with the words "civic duty."

"Wow. What a saint. Sounds like Mrs. Blankenship's untimely demise was her pot of gold at the end of the rainbow."

"Exactly. But, Tess, she wants Evie! She said I had no business with a show dog like Evie, and ordered me to hand her over."

"What? No way."

"Evie is Mrs. Blankenship's top-ranking dog. I'm afraid Darlene will stop at nothing to get her."

"What are you going to do?"

"I don't know. She threatened to sue me for custody." This week alone, I'd had more threats of lawsuits than in my three years of practice.

"Who sues over custody of a dog? Can she even do that?"

"I guess you can pretty much sue anyone for anything if you can find a lawyer to take the case."

"What about Mr. Granger? Could he help?"

"He's a criminal defense attorney, Tess, not a dog custody lawyer."

"Well, he's still a lawyer. He probably knows how to use Google and do lawyer stuff like write cease-and-desist letters. You could ask him."

She had a point. A lawyer was a lawyer, after all, and Mr. Granger was the only legal authority I knew.

"I'm more worried that if she killed Mrs. Blankenship just to get her dogs, she wouldn't hesitate to do the same to me if I don't fork over Evie."

"Amy, this is really freaking me out. Why don't you just give her the dog?"

"I can't! You wouldn't believe how horrible she treats her dogs. Evie finally trusts me, now. I couldn't do that to her."

Tess plopped into the desk chair, her leg jiggling with nervous energy. I could tell she was deep in thought. "Maybe you can tell her some long-lost relative came and took Evie."

"Then Darlene will want to know why the long-lost relative didn't want the other dogs."

"Oh, right." She nibbled on her lower lip. "Then you need to go to the police and tell them of your suspicion. If they arrest her for the murder, you can keep Evie. Not to mention clear your name."

Panic at the idea of stepping back into the police station wrapped around my throat like chilly fingers. What if they'd forgotten about me being a suspect, and my reappearance at the police station reminded them, and they grabbed me and locked me in a cell?

But Tess was right. If the police didn't know Darlene had an excellent motive for wanting Mildred out of the way, someone should enlighten them. That "someone" being me. Besides, the police needed to look at someone other than me. And the more I thought about it, Darlene wouldn't have appeared out of place hanging around Mrs. B's coffee thermos. She belonged in the Chihuahua area.

I drew in a long breath. "Okay. I'll call Officer Lang right now."

Tess beamed at me and made no move to leave as I reached for the phone. I handed her Corky and gave her my classic raised eyebrows/head tilt combination until she took the hint.

"Fine. I don't know why I can't stay. Calling the cops was my idea. I just want to make sure you don't forget something important."

"I appreciate it, Tess, but I can't think straight if you're watching me."

She flounced out the door, letting it bang behind her.

I removed Lang's card from my purse and punched in the number. To my surprise, he answered on the first ring.

"Uh, hi," I said, not quite sure where to start. "This is Amy Dixon. Remember?" *Stupid question. Of course, he remembers you. He held you in the interrogation room for hours.*

"Yes, Dr. Dixon, what can I do for you?"

"Well, uh, I found out something about Darlene McDougal that I thought you should know."

"You don't say?" His voice took on a mocking tone. "And just what might that be?"

His scornful response struck a raw nerve, and my temper overrode my terror. How dare he be snarky? What I had to say was important. Didn't the police rely on tips from the public all the time to help them solve cases?

"It just so happens that she was intensely jealous of Mrs. Blankenship's show dogs. And now that Mrs. B's dead, guess who took her dogs?"

"Darlene McDougal."

"That's right," I said, ramming my point home. "Doesn't that strike you as just a tad convenient?"

"And you know this how?"

Uh-oh. Still, I hadn't done anything wrong. Best to be upfront with the policeman, even if it *did* make me sound like a nosy busybody.

"Because I took a puppy I just bought to her house to ask for advice from a professional breeder, and happened to see Mrs. Blankenship's dogs. Darlene told me she'd taken them in."

"Uh-huh. And what made you seek out Mrs. McDougal's advice instead of someone else's?"

I bristled. "Because she's a well-known breeder, that's why."

"And who did you buy the puppy from?"

All my bluster flew out the window. "Mrs. Papadopoulos," I admitted.

"Dr. Dixon, are you, in some way, attempting to interfere in an active police investigation?"

My stomach did a back flip. "No! Of course not."

"Good, because I could charge you with interference if that were the case."

This conversation was not going the way I'd envisioned.

He continued, "By the way, Martin Billings complained that you'd been by to see him on the pretense of wanting training for your dog, but somehow wound up asking him questions about the murder. He thought you might be insinuating that he did it."

"What's wrong with my wanting dog training?" I huffed. "And as for the questions, he totally misunderstood. It's only natural that people who were at the fairgrounds on Saturday would talk about the murder."

Lang grunted. "Uh-huh. It just seems . . . odd that you've had reason to interact with three of the four people you observed having a public spat with the victim."

My mouth opened. Closed. I had no comeback.

"Dr. Dixon, let me be perfectly clear. Stay out of this investigation. I know on television, amateur sleuths solve the crime for the police all the time. This isn't television. This is real life. The police aren't as clueless as you think. And you could be placing yourself in danger. You just stick to giving rabies shots and spaying cats and leave the detective work to actual detectives." Something he said clicked in my brain. If I could be placing myself in danger, did that mean I had slipped from the top of the suspect list?

With as humble a tone as I could possibly muster, I cleared my throat and said, "Does that mean I'm no longer a suspect?"

"I didn't say that. As a matter of fact, I didn't say anything except to stay out of this. Got it?"

"Yes, sir." I desperately wanted to rehash the overwhelming evidence against Darlene McDougal to be sure he understood how guilty she looked, but I decided not to push it. "Thank you." I disconnected the call.

"How did it go?" Tess asked when I came out of the office.

"He told me to stay out of the investigation." I sighed. "I only wish I knew where to find Trudy."

Chapter Eighteen

As it turned out, I didn't have to hunt Trudy down. She practically fell into my lap. Imagine my surprise when I walked into the exam room later that morning to find the very woman I needed to question standing across the table from me. The young, attractive brunette shifted from one foot to the other, her eyes darting all over the room.

"Hello," I greeted, playing it cool and holding out my hand. "I'm Dr. Amy Dixon."

"Trudy Snodgrass," she said, giving my hand a firm squeeze, although I noted her palm was sweaty. "And this is Bentley." She gestured to a carrier sitting on the table in which a beautifully marked tan and white Chihuahua with caramel-colored eyes peered through the grate with suspicion.

"Nice looking little guy. What can I do for you, Ms. Snodgrass?"

"Trudy, please." She opened the crate and pulled out the infamous three-thousand-dollar, epileptic Bentley. "To be honest, I saw you at the dog show the other day, and I thought I'd get a second opinion."

"Oh?" I thought I feigned ignorance pretty well. "A second opinion about what?"

"Bentley has seizures." Her face clouded.

"I'm sorry to hear that. Does he take anti-convulsant medication?" I ran my hand over his round head, feeling an open fontanelle, or "soft spot." Bentley stiffened and regarded me with wary eyes.

"Yes, phenobarbital."

"Does that help with the seizures?"

"Yes. Since he started the medication, he's only had one mild seizure."

"Well, that's good," I said, shining my penlight into his buggy eyes, and observing a normal pupillary light response and normally directed globes. Tilting his head up, down, right, and left, I verified that Bentley had normal eye movement. I ran through all his cranial nerves, then flipped up his lip and noted normal gum color and an underbite.

"My other vet said Bentley has hydrocephalus, which is causing the seizures." She made the statement with the kind of doom that usually accompanies something dire.

"That's possible." I palpated Bentley's lymph nodes and listened to his heart, which pounded away in a rapid, steady rhythm. Bentley stared stoically ahead as if he could make me disappear by ignoring me.

I stepped back and slung my stethoscope around my neck. "Does Bentley have difficulty learning, or seem mentally dull?"

"No, not at all. He's extremely smart. He passed all his obedience training with flying colors." Pride colored her tone.

"Did your other vet do any lab work on Bentley?"

"Yes, he did blood work." She pulled a sheaf of papers from her purse.

I scanned the routine blood tests, finding them to be normal. "Well, it looks like we can rule out other causes of seizures, like low blood sugar or liver disease. But blood tests can't definitively tell whether a seizure is due to hydrocephalus, idiopathic epilepsy, or something else."

"How can you tell if hydrocephalus is the cause?"

"Dogs with clinical signs related to hydrocephalus often, but not always, have a dull mental state and abnormal behavior, like walking in circles or pressing their heads into corners. They may have trouble house-breaking or learning."

I palpated Bentley's abdomen, which was a bit tense, most likely from his stress from being at the vet's office, but found nothing abnormal. He cast a glance at the closed door, and I could hear the wheels of his brain turning to find ways of escaping.

"To be sure, I would have to refer you to a neurology specialist for advanced imaging and other tests, like an electroencephalogram and possibly a spinal tap."

Worry lines creased her forehead. "I'm afraid I don't have that kind of money."

"As long as the phenobarbital controls his seizures and he's clinically normal, there's no necessity for additional testing, other than running a phenobarbital blood level every six months. It looks like his last level was within the normal range, so there's no need to adjust his dose."

"What if the phenobarbital stops working?"

I ran my hands over the dog's joints, pleased to

find he had normal patellas, which were often luxated in his breed. "There are several other medications we can try. My advice is to continue doing what's working. Many dogs with seizures live perfectly normal lives if the seizures can be controlled. It doesn't stop them from being happy, healthy pets."

"Pets." She bit out the word as though it were repugnant. Then she picked up Bentley and cradled him under her chin. "I love Bentley, but I bought him for breeding."

I schooled my features into a mask of professional neutrality. "Oh, I'm sorry. But we don't recommend breeding dogs with seizures, as a genetic component may be involved."

Her shoulders slumped, and she sighed. "That's what my other vet said."

"I'm sorry," I repeated. "It looks like I'm just confirming what you were already told."

Her frustration spilled out. "I paid three thousand dollars for this dog," she said bitterly. "To show and use as a breeder. The woman I bought him from assured me I could make a lot of money."

"Wow. I can understand how disappointing that must be."

"Yeah, and she won't . . . wouldn't give me a refund. Even a partial refund would have helped, but now she's dead."

I couldn't have asked for a better opening. "You don't mean Mildred Blankenship? The lady who died at the dog show on Saturday?"

She fixed me with a penetrating stare, full of unsettling curiosity. "That's the one," she said in a tone sharp enough to cut glass. "I'm sorry she died and all, but it doesn't excuse the fact that she refused to do right by me by selling me a dog I can't breed."

I leaned in and lowered my voice. "Mildred was murdered, you know."

"So I heard." Her angry expression changed to one of intrigue. "They say someone put poison in her coffee." She kissed the top of Bentley's head.

"I heard that, too." I watched her face for any incriminating signs.

She looked around as though several people crowded the small exam room, and said in a soft, conspiratorial manner, "Do you know what kind of poison it was?"

I hesitated, not particularly wanting to share the fact that I knew about the phenobarbital. *My* phenobarbital. The fewer people who knew where the drug came from, the better.

"No," I lied.

She studied me in a way that made me uncomfortable. I ducked my head and jotted some notes in Bentley's chart to avoid her piercing gaze, then said nonchalantly, "You were there that day. Did you see anything suspicious?"

Trudy shook her head. "No, but I was pretty upset, so I didn't pay much attention to anything else going on around me. And I left soon after I talked to Mildred that morning." She locked eyes with me again. "Did *you* see anything suspicious?"

I pushed out what I hoped was a believable laugh. "I'm afraid not. I was too busy to notice much of anything." I switched topics. "You said you took Bentley to obedience classes. Was it with Martin Billings? I met him at the dog show, and I just bought a new puppy I want to have trained."

Horror registered on her face. "Gracious no! That man isn't even a certified trainer."

Oh? That *was interesting.* "Really? I had no idea." Nick had told me that Billings had been Mrs. B's handler up until last year. How could she not have known she'd entrusted her dogs to an unreputable, uncertified trainer? Didn't she have her finger on the pulse of all things dog? Maybe that's why she refused to pay him. And, although I didn't hear her say so, perhaps she'd even threatened to expose him. Exposure of his secret could certainly be a motive for murder. Marty's suspect status jumped back up neck-and-neck with Darlene's.

"Go to Shady Oaks Kennel. They have a top-notch trainer."

"Thanks, I'll keep that in mind."

Trudy put Bentley back in his crate. "Thank you for your time, Dr. Dixon."

"Amy. Despite everything, Bentley is a great little dog."

A sad smile touched her lips. "Yes, he is."

I walked to the door and opened it for her. "If there's any way I can help you, please don't hesitate to ask." I handed her my card with my cell number on it.

As Trudy exited, she turned and said, "I'd like to transfer Bentley's records to you, if that's okay."

"Of course. I'd be happy to be Bentley's vet. Just tell the receptionist when you leave, and she can call your previous vet for his records."

"Thanks, I'll do that."

She disappeared around the corner into the lobby. I felt a small gratification that Trudy had been comfortable enough with me to want to change veterinarians. Although flattered, I couldn't help but wonder why she chose to leave her previous vet and whether or not it had anything to do with Mrs. B's murder. But unless she volunteered that information, I was in the dark.

I hustled to the back, nearly slipping in a large puddle of water, to find Tess elbow-deep in suds, scrubbing a grumpy-looking Shih Tzu that clearly didn't appreciate spa day.

"Do you know who I just saw?"

Her hand stopped in mid-shampoo, covered in a cloud of frothy bubbles. "Who?"

"Trudy! The one suspect we couldn't track down."

Tess' eyes grew wide, and she let go of the dog's tail, which wagged indignantly, spraying us with soap and water. "You mean she just walked in out of the blue?"

I grabbed a towel and wiped my face. "Yes. Supposedly to seek a second opinion on Bentley's seizures, but it seemed to me like she had more on her agenda than just that."

Tess placed one hand back on the dog and rubbed her face on her other sleeve. "What do you mean?"

"I'm not sure. I can't quite put my finger on it, but it seemed like she was questioning *me* as much as I was questioning her."

"What did she want to know?"

"She asked if I knew what poison killed Mrs. Blankenship. I told her no, but it didn't look like she believed me. She also wanted to know if I saw anything suspicious."

Tess seemed to realize the dog in the tub wasn't

getting any cleaner and resumed her scrubbing. "Do you think Trudy might be the killer?"

I blew out a defeated breath. "I don't know. At this point, I don't know who to suspect."

Tess picked up the sprayer and began hosing off the shampoo. The dog growled and snapped at the water. "What now?"

"I wonder if the police have managed to figure out who Trudy is." I grabbed the edge of the counter for support, suddenly feeling like I might topple over from the weight of everything. "Do you think I should tell them? Or should I keep quiet? After the warning I got from Officer Lang this morning, the last thing I need is another lecture. Or for him to take a closer look at me."

She reached for a towel and wrapped it around the Shih Tzu. "I get it, but seriously, what's the alternative? Let Trudy vanish into thin air again?"

"Well, at least I have a last name and an address, so unless she decides to skip town, I've got a way to track her down."

"True, but I still think you should call the police."

I cringed at the idea of knotting Officer Lang's knickers any more than I already had. But what if the police couldn't find Trudy on their own?

Chapter Nineteen

I whipped out my phone and snapped a picture of Trudy from her client application photo. We routinely kept pictures of clients and pets to jog our memories of who they were. Plus, you'd be surprised how many people resemble their dogs. Or vice-versa. I texted Nick the picture to see if he knew her.

His reply came instantly. "Sorry, I don't know her and don't remember seeing her on Saturday."

I frowned at the screen. Drat. Not only had my lead hit a dead end, but now that all the suspects had been questioned, Nick had no excuse to hang out with me anymore. Unless I gave him one.

Did I dare to be presumptuous? Normally, I wasn't a forward person. I'd mastered the art of passive longing from afar, but with Nick, I could make an exception. I started to type, "Dinner tonight?" but stopped when I saw the words, "Nick is typing" pop up on my screen.

His message came through. "How about dinner tonight? We can take a break from sleuthing for an evening."

My heart flopped around like a dying fish in my chest. "Sounds good," I typed. "My place? I'll cook."

What in the name of all things holy possessed me to say *that*? I wasn't exactly a culinary wizard. My cooking skills were more "microwave magician" than "master chef." Ordinarily, I didn't regard my lack of cooking expertise as a big deal. I had other talents, such as being able to draw blood from a parakeet and reciting all the books of the Bible in order. Talents that lacked relevance when faced with a hungry, handsome man expecting me to make good on my promise to feed him dinner.

"Great. See you around six?"

"Six is fine." I added XOXO for "hugs and kisses," and then deleted it. There was forward, and then there was *forward*. No sense in scaring the man away when I still held pretend girlfriend status. I still held out hope of moving out of pretend territory.

Maybe I could stop somewhere, get take-out, and pass it off as homemade. No, that would be dishonest. I snorted. It wasn't as though the two of us hadn't spent the entire week being less than truthful. But just to other people, not to each other.

Spaghetti. Spaghetti was hard to mess up, and everyone liked spaghetti, right? Unless Nick was anti-pasta, in which case, looks or no looks, not liking pasta would be a dealbreaker. I needed to run home at lunch to be sure I had everything I needed for tonight.

On an impulse, I brought Sierra and Evie back to the clinic with me for the afternoon. I'd been gone so many nights this past week, I felt guilty for neglecting them, especially with Evie still trying to acclimate to a new place. Maybe I'd give them both a bath, spruce them up for Nick's visit. Sierra was beginning to smell a little "doggy."

Between afternoon appointments, my thoughts kept circling back to Trudy. Should I call Officer Lang and risk his wrath for sticking my nose where it didn't belong again? In the end, I finally decided the police needed Trudy's contact information. I reached for the phone and punched in his number. When it went straight to voicemail, I exhaled a sigh of relief, like someone who'd just defused a bomb.

"Hi, this is Amy Dixon again." I tried to make my voice sound upbeat and innocent. "I know you told me to stay out of this investigation, and I am, I swear. But I had a new client today, and it turned out to be Trudy, the woman who is upset about the puppy Mrs. Blankenship sold her." My words began to spill out faster than water from a busted faucet as I raced to relay all the important details before voicemail cut me off. Having a tendency to babble when I'm nervous, I'm sure I sounded like someone auditioning for an auctioneer competition. But Lang was a smart man. He'd figure it out, hopefully before his knickers got too twisty.

I put Trudy, Officer Lang, and all things murder-related out of my head as I focused on finishing up my appointments. Well, to be perfectly truthful, I focused on getting home and preparing a perfect dinner while going through the motions at work. Fortunately, the rest of the afternoon was slow—until ten minutes before closing, when an emergency hit by car dog came through the door. Not alone, of course. His frantic owners accompanied him.

My adrenaline kicked in, and my brain blocked out

everything but stabilizing the accident victim in front of me. I made my initial assessment, placed an IV line, administered fluids, took radiographs, and ultrasounded his belly. After ruling out internal bleeding, ruptured bladder, pneumothorax, and fractures, I administered pain medication, cleaned up the road rash on his legs, and applied bandages. Then I advised the clients to take the dog to the overnight emergency clinic for monitoring.

By the time I made it home, it was almost six, and I knew I had to rush to change clothes, brush my tangled hair, and scrub the residual blood off my arms. Not to mention putting a pot of water on to boil. I reached my door, suddenly realizing that I'd forgotten Sierra and Evie in all the excitement. Oh, poor things! What must they be thinking about my abandoning them? I'd have to explain to Nick that dinner would be a little late.

I unlocked my front door and froze. The scene before me was mass mayhem with overturned furniture, drawers yanked out with the contents dumped, and my couch cushions scattered. A broken picture frame lay face down near the wall, with shards of glass catching the late afternoon sun through the sliding glass door. Cabinets had been rummaged through and left open. The crushing sense of violation rooted me to the spot, my feet glued to the floor.

Chapter Twenty

Yes, in retrospect, I should have run screaming out the door, called 911, and maybe armed myself with the rabies pole in case the intruder still lurked inside. But I couldn't move. My feet had apparently fused to the floor. My chest tightened with the realization of my home invasion, and wrenching sobs broke free as I stared helplessly at the desecration of my castle.

I didn't even hear Nick approach until he materialized beside me, nearly scaring me out of what was left of my wits.

"Amy? What's . . . Oh my gosh!"

Words wouldn't slide through my closed-off throat. I turned and, without even thinking about what I was doing, fell into his arms, drenching his shirt with my hot tears. He patted my back with one hand while simultaneously pulling his cell phone from his pocket with the other.

"Police," I heard him say, his voice tense and controlled. A sense of unreality smothered me like a heavy blanket while I listened to the one-sided conversation. "Someone broke into my girlfriend's house at 105 Poplar Street." A pause. "I don't think so." Another pause. "We're outside on the porch." A final pause. "Yes, I understand. Thank you."

Even the words "my girlfriend's house" failed to work their magic and penetrate my shock.

"The police are on their way." He pocketed the phone and led me to the porch swing, where he pulled me down beside him and continued to hold me as he set the swing in motion with a slow push from his foot. "They said not to go inside until they get here."

I sniffed loudly and wiped my eyes on my sleeve, my mascara surely creating an abstract masterpiece on my face. The hot mess of my face should have humiliated me in front of the one man I wanted to impress, but I couldn't bring myself to care. "Why would anyone do such a thing?" My voice came out trembling and raw.

"I don't know. Maybe you struck a nerve with someone."

"But what could they possibly be looking for?" My nose betrayed me with a particularly undignified sniffle, and I wiped it on my sleeve, too. Again, not caring.

He removed his arm and sat up suddenly, an urgency creeping into his voice. "Amy, where are the dogs?"

Relief flooded over me for the first time since I'd walked through the door. "At the clinic." Thank goodness they hadn't been at home! Sierra wasn't exactly a guard dog—more of a hide-under-the-bed-and-pray-the-burglar-doesn't-see-me type of dog. And Evie? Well, all four pounds of her couldn't do much to stop a burglar, unless her trembling caused an earthquake. "I took them to work with me this afternoon, and then there was a late emergency and . . ." I was babbling again.

I reached into my bag and scooped out Corky, my other, poor, forgotten fur baby. "Oh, sweetie." I sniffled into his soft black fur.

Nick apparently deciphered my rambling. "That's good. Who knows what might have happened if they had been here?" His normally easygoing expression turned deadly serious. "Or you."

I hadn't thought about *that*. A chill skittered down my spine. My house—the one place meant to be safe—felt anything but. Installing an alarm system rose to the top of my to-do list. And/or getting a Rottweiler.

We sat in silence, the gentle rocking and creaking of the swing calming my frazzled nerves. Until the flashing blue lights lit up my driveway. And out of the police cruiser emerged Officer Lang himself.

I let out a groan.

"Dr. Dixon," he said by way of greeting, "why are you always on the wrong side of trouble?" He crossed his arms and regarded me with a stern expression.

I gritted my teeth. "Is this town so small that you have to do everything yourself?"

"I was in the neighborhood."

"Lucky me," I muttered under my breath. "Look, this break-in is hardly my fault. I'm the victim, here, remember?"

He opened his mouth as if to spout off a cutting retort, then closed it again and exhaled sharply. "Wait here until I clear the premises."

"Go ahead. You're familiar with my house," I said, unable to stop the sarcasm edging into my voice. Of all the police on the Claymore County police force, why did I always get stuck with Officer Lang? The man brought out the devil in me.

Lang gave me a look, the kind that made me wish I'd made more of an effort to be nice. He was there to help, after all. He disappeared into the house, and Nick and I settled back onto the swing like two prisoners awaiting sentencing.

Time stretched on like an eternity, each second slower than the last, until Lang finally reappeared.

"It's clear. Whoever did this is long gone." He gave me a hard-to-read expression. Annoyance? Pity? Guilty as charged? "I need you to walk through the house and see if anything's missing."

I took a deep breath, steeling myself for the ordeal of examining the degree of my violation. Nick slid his fingers between mine, infusing me with warmth and courage.

We stepped inside, and I surveyed the wreckage of my once-cozy sanctuary. Nick set about righting furniture and gathering strewn drawer contents in an effort to restore some semblance of order. He stacked pillows carefully as if aesthetics could somehow undo the defilement of my space.

Despite the chaos, nothing appeared to be missing. My television and laptop remained in their place. Nothing of value lived in the drawers. I moved into my bedroom next, and although the drawers had been rifled through, my few pieces of jewelry and the money in my spare change jar looked undisturbed. The bathroom and guest bedroom remained largely intact, and other than cabinets being flung open in the kitchen, nothing was broken.

I turned in a slow circle, taking in the senseless

intrusion. "I don't understand. They didn't take anything valuable. So, what did they want? And how did they get in?"

"They jimmied the sliding glass door to the back yard," said Officer Lang, leading me to the back of the house. "Those doors are easy to force open. You might want to get a broomstick to place in the track. Or, better yet, an alarm system."

I nodded. "After this, I guess I'll have to." However, I had no idea where I would get the money for an expensive alarm system.

"Since nothing seems to be missing, we can probably rule out robbery as the motive." Lang's stare sharpened, leveling me with the weight of his words. "Dr. Dixon, I hope that after this incident, you will back off from playing amateur detective. I don't think this was a random break-in. I think you rattled someone's cage, and now you're putting yourself in danger. Promise me you'll stay away from the people you've already talked to. We can't protect you if you deliberately keep putting yourself in harm's way."

His warning settled in my chest like a lead weight. But, in all fairness, if the police hadn't initially targeted me as their prime suspect, I wouldn't have had to take matters into my own hands. I was dying to ask if they were closing in on someone else, but my inner common sense advised me not to.

"I promise." And for once, I actually meant it.

He studied me like a man weighing the truth behind my words, but apparently deciding to let it go, gave a curt nod.

"All right." He glanced at Nick, then back at me. "Call if you need me."

"Thank you, Officer," said Nick, ushering him to the door and closing it firmly behind him.

I remained standing, stuck somewhere between dazed and exhausted. I'd just been robbed—except nothing had actually been stolen. Instead, someone had deliberately torn through my house, making a mess for seemingly no reason. Was someone trying to send me a warning? If so, who? And what were they warning me against?

"I guess this means you didn't cook dinner," Nick quipped, and his effort at lifting me out of the deep funk into which I'd sunk sent a laugh tumbling from my lips.

Plopping onto the sofa—now restored, thanks to Nick—I sighed. "You got me there." Then, with a sudden surge of emotion and gratitude, I said, "I'm sorry, Nick. For everything. For getting you mixed up in this awful mess and . . . well, everything."

He settled next to me and reached for my hand, rubbing his thumb along the back, sending shivers up my arm. "I'm not. We're in this together. If nothing else, I've got to spend time with you. I don't regret anything, except for what you're going through."

My silly heart went berserk. "Does this mean—"

"When all this murder stuff is over," he interrupted, "I'd still like to hang around with you, if that's okay."

I grinned like a lunatic. "I guess that would be okay. But I don't know what we'll do for excitement."

He chuckled. "Excitement's way overrated."

"I'm beginning to think you're right."

He let out a dramatic sigh and said, "Since it appears you're not going to make good on your promise to cook me dinner, why don't I take you out? Then we'll stop by the clinic and get the dogs."

I nodded, already halfway to grabbing my purse when he added, "On one condition."

I stopped. "What?"

"Go wash your face first. I don't want to be seen with a woman who looks like she went a few rounds with Muhammad Ali. People might judge me."

Horrors! My hands flew to my face as if I didn't want him to see me. As if he already hadn't. I dashed into the bathroom, nearly tripping on my own feet, and stared into the mirror. The reflection staring back at me was worse than I'd imagined—red, puffy eyes, and streaks of mascara dripping down my cheeks like a clown in mourning.

I splashed cold water on my face, scrubbing at the evidence of my emotional breakdown. Makeup remover helped erase the black streaks, but I still looked rough. A little concealer and powder worked wonders, though, and I managed to pull off looking semi-human again.

Then I glanced down at my scrubs, covered in hair and blood and who knows what else, and decided a change of clothes would go a long way to enhance my overall attractiveness score. I rummaged through my closet, pulled out a pair of white jeans and a turquoise top, and hurriedly discarded my soiled scrubs for a fresh outfit. As I slipped my feet into sequined sandals, something green on the floor caught my eye.

I bent to examine the strange object. And froze, for the second time this evening. Gripping it between my thumb and forefinger, I recognized it as a fake, neon green fingernail, just like Darlene McDougal wore. My initial shock turned into white-hot fury. Darlene had invaded my home and destroyed my peace.

Ragged, angry breaths poured through my lips. I stomped out into the living room, the green fingernail wrapped in my clenched fist. Nick looked up, startled, as I pushed past him, snatched my purse and keys, and marched out the front door.

"Amy! Where are you going?" Nick raced after me.

"To kill Darlene McDougal."

Chapter Twenty-One

My rage frightened me, but I was completely powerless under its control. I yanked open my truck door and climbed inside, slamming the door with enough force to rattle the windows.

"What?" Nick ran around to the passenger side and jumped in, his expression a mix of confusion and concern. "What are you talking about?"

"It was her," I said through tight lips.

"Her what?"

"She's the one who broke into my house. And I intend to find out why." I slammed the gear shift into reverse and squealed out of the driveway, as Nick struggled to fasten his seat belt. Mine remained defiantly unbuckled.

"How do you know?" he asked, his voice rising.

"I found this." I opened my fisted right hand to reveal the green fingernail, as I steered with my left. "Recognize it? Who do we know who has fake green fingernails?"

Nick gently took the incriminating evidence from my hand, his brows furrowing. "Where did you find this?"

"On the floor of my bedroom closet." I did a California rolling stop at the stop sign and pressed the accelerator to the floor.

"Okay, she's the one who broke in. But we need to call the police."

"No! I'm going to have it out with her. Nobody does this to me!" My foot pressed harder on the gas, the truck skidding as I took a curve too fast.

"Amy! Slow down, you're going to cause an accident."

I could feel Nick's eyes on me, imploring me, but the need to throttle Darlene outweighed all common sense.

"Be reasonable. If she's the killer, we can't just confront her. She could be dangerous. Let me call Officer Lang." He reached into his pocket, then groaned. "I took my phone out to send a text while you were changing, and I left it on the coffee table when you came running out."

I glanced over at him briefly, my grip tightening on the steering wheel.

"Amy, please stop."

The thought occurred to me that my irrational behavior might send Nick scurrying away from the crazy lady for good. Even I didn't recognize myself. But I couldn't stop. A force stronger than my good judgment propelled me forward. If the police wanted to charge me for Mrs. B's murder, they might as well tack on Darlene's, too. A murderer could only serve so many life sentences.

As I jerked the truck into Darlene's driveway, gravel shot out behind me like buckshot. It suddenly occurred to me that I might be dragging Nick into felony territory by making him an accessory to the murder I was about to commit.

"You can wait in the truck if you want," I said, throwing open the door. I didn't bother to close it.

I stormed up to Darlene's door, homicide in my heart and Nick on my heels, and jabbed the doorbell several times.

"All right, already, I'm coming." Darlene opened the door, and shock registered on her face at the sight of me. She quickly recovered her composure and went on the offensive, planting a hand on her hip and leaning against the door jamb. "What do you want?" she snapped.

Not waiting for an invitation, I barged in. She stumbled back, more surprised than angry, which told me a lot. I stood nose-to-nose with her in the foyer. The chorus of a herd of Chihuahuas sang to us from the back of the house.

"How dare you break into my house!" I spit out.

Her penciled-in eyebrows rose in indignation. "Break into your house? Have you completely lost your mind?"

"Don't even go there, Darlene," I growled. "I have proof." That's when I realized I *didn't* have the proof. I turned to Nick and shot him a "look." He stepped forward and produced the lone green fingernail like it was Exhibit A.

"Recognize this, Darlene?" My eyes flew to her hands, which she was attempting to shove into her jeans' pockets. Without thinking, I grabbed both her wrists and yanked them into the light before they disappeared out of sight. There was the convicting evidence—ten fake neon green nails minus one. Her right index finger stood naked, shamed and exposed.

Her posture deflated like a party balloon. "Okay, I admit it," she mumbled, slumping against the wall.

Her admission caused something inside me to shift, and my anger abated ever so slightly. "Why?" Bewilderment replaced my wrathful tone.

"I wanted Evangelina Rose." She covered her face with her mangled manicure like a toddler playing peekaboo with the truth.

"What?" My voice hit an octave normally reserved for opera singers. Disbelief overrode all anger, now, leaving me drained.

"I'm sorry," she sniffled. Her hands still covered her face, making her words blurred. "She's so perfect."

"She's a *dog,* Darlene," Nick said.

"You don't understand. She's a perfect show dog. A true champion."

Too stunned for words, I simply stood there as her shoulders began to heave.

"Why did you trash Amy's house?" asked Nick.

"I don't know." She collapsed to the floor, drawing her bony knees up to her chest. She finally pulled her hands away from her face, tears streaming from her eyes. "I just lost it when she wasn't there. I guess I just went a little—"

"Crazy?" Nick supplied helpfully.

She gulped, her Adam's apple bobbing in her throat, and nodded, her eyes glistening with unshed tears. "I don't know what came over me. I'm not proud of what I did."

I saw a crack in her armor. Time to press for an all-out confession. "Is that why you killed Mildred?

Because you coveted her show dogs?"

Her jaw dropped and her eyes widened in surprise. "I didn't kill Mildred. Are you insane? How could you even suggest such a thing?"

"You broke into Amy's house with the intention of stealing a dog. It seems pretty obvious you'd do anything to get your hands on Evie," Nick said.

I shot him a grateful look. Despite how we'd wound up here, Nick had my back.

"Yeah," I echoed. "Did you want Evie badly enough to kill Mildred for her?"

"Breaking into a house and murdering someone are two completely different things," she sputtered.

"Yet both constitute criminal activity, which you have shown you are more than capable of." I glared at her, willing her to come clean.

She stretched out her green-manicured hands minus one traitorous nail, palms up. "You have to believe me. I didn't kill Mildred. I swear by my dogs' lives."

"Why should we believe anything you say? I'm calling the police." I reached into my bag and pulled out my phone.

"No! Wait!" she cried. "I'm sorry for what I did to your house. I'll pay for any damages. And . . . and I won't try to take Evangelina Rose from you. Just please, please don't call the police."

I hesitated, my finger hovering over the buttons.

"My husband will absolutely kill me if he finds out what I did. He already thinks I'm too obsessed with my dogs."

I had to say I agreed with the man. But there was already too much killing going on. "I should report you."

"Please. I know I did a terrible thing. But I would never *kill* anyone."

I blew out a breath. "All right. I'll send you a bill for damages, and I won't tell the police. For now. But I can't promise they won't question you about Mildred's murder." I wondered if I'd just made a huge mistake.

Nick shook his head. "Let's go."

I allowed him to take my hand and lead me out the door, leaving Darlene in a soggy heap on the floor. Once we reached the truck, I turned around, put my hands on either side of my mouth, and called, "And for the record, Darlene, I wouldn't breed Corky to one of your dogs if he were the last Chihuahua on Earth."

Nick's attempt to suppress a chuckle failed. "Give me the keys," he said, and I relinquished them without protest.

Once we'd reached the main road, I broke the silence. "Thank you again. I'm sorry I went all Lizzie Borden back there."

He shot me a crooked grin. "Well, at least you didn't chop Darlene into pieces. I suppose not having an axe at your fingertips might have helped avert that crisis. But do you think it was a good idea to let her off the hook so easily?"

I sighed. "I don't know." I rubbed my fingers between my brows, where a headache threatened to break forth in full jackhammer glory. "I guess there's no real harm done. And I don't have to worry about her coming after Evie again."

"Unless she murders you next."

Chapter Twenty-Two

I would have loved to spend the next day, Saturday, basking in Nick's charm and beautiful eyes, with no agenda for investigating a murder, but alas, duty called. By duty, I mean family obligations. I guess even men whose idea of fun was hanging around with me and the mess that had become my life had mothers to visit and casseroles to endure. I had yet to wow Nick with my qualities as a domestic goddess. I'll bet his mother was a great cook.

I couldn't quite blame him for keeping me at arm's length from his probably normal family. But to be fair, up until a week ago, I had lived a normal, boring life that he knew nothing about. His absence left a Nick-shaped hole in my day. I had gotten used to his presence the way one gets used to a comfortable shoe or a good Wi-fi signal. Now the day stretched before me like a Netflix marathon—full of potential, but utterly unsatisfying.

Determined not to sink into a spiral of daytime television and passive-aggressive cleaning, I settled in the kitchen with a legal pad and my purple gel pen. Productivity would take my mind off Nick. First on the agenda was drafting a charge sheet for the damage

Darlene had done to my house. I itemized every injury with righteous indignation.

1. Broken Dollar General Store picture frame: $1.99 plus tax.
2. Replacement patio door lock: $45.00 (Okay, that was an estimate, as I had no idea what the replacement lock for the old, rusty, warped one cost.)

What else? I desperately wanted to bring the total to $1000 to pay off Corky. What did lawyers charge for pain and suffering?

3. Emotional trauma from an almost dognapping: Incalculable.
4. My peace of mind: Priceless.
5. Time spent straightening up the mess: $900/hour.

If I estimated a little higher for the cost of the patio lock, I could reach my goal, the price of a Chihuahua puppy. Karma, Darlene, for calling my puppy ugly. I stared at the paper for a long moment. Then, after much internal debate, I tore it up. I couldn't, in good Christian conscience, extort hush money out of someone—even if she did try to steal my dog and maybe commit a murder. The damages were minimal, and although annoying, hardly added up to a grand. Besides, everyone knows that once you start blackmailing a murderer, you're next.

Darlene had given a pretty convincing performance in declaring her innocence of Mrs. B's death. But, I reminded myself, she'd also tried to snow me by denying everything when I confronted her about the break-in, so I couldn't completely trust her.

I pulled a fresh piece of paper and scrawled "Suspects" across the top, underlining it three times. Below that, I wrote their names and motives, like a game of Clue.

1. Martin Billings: The deceased owed him a lot of money, which she refused to pay. Plus, he held no certification as a dog trainer. That fact, in and of itself, didn't necessarily disqualify him from training dogs, as certification wasn't a legal requirement. But a certified trainer held more credibility with certain circles, such as breeders and dog show people.

2. Joanna Papadopoulos: The deceased had bad-mouthed her, sullying her reputation. Joanna had guided and mentored Mildred, who showed her appreciation by stabbing Joanna in the back. Mildred had also caused her to lose a puppy sale. But Joanna hadn't seemed terribly upset. Still, she might be one of those people who could transform from Jekyll to Hyde in a heartbeat. I *had* observed her Hyde side.

3. Darlene McDougal: Bitter rivalry and jealousy of the deceased. She'd taken Mildred's dogs faster than you could say "AKC registration" after Mildred's death, and wanted Evie so badly she was willing to

commit a crime to get her. Plus, she was a horrible woman. Just sayin'.

4. Trudy Snodgrass: Extremely upset because the puppy that the deceased had sold her turned out to be unusable for breeding, and then brushed her off, refusing a refund.

I studied the motives carefully, weighing each as to level of significance. But my idea of significance might differ from someone else's. Of all the motives, I found Trudy's to be the weakest. No one could foretell what medical problems a puppy might develop down the line, and unless Mildred had knowingly and deceptively bred dogs with epilepsy, she couldn't be held accountable, even if she could have been more empathetic. However, Trudy didn't strike me as the poster child for rational thinking. Trudy could have gone from livid to lethal. Rage has a way of clouding common sense, as I'd learned the hard way last night.

Money, however, was a classic motive for murder. Maybe a ten grand motive. Besides, Martin Billings was a real snake who gave me the willies. Under that slick, too smooth exterior, he gave me the vibes of someone who'd sabotage your brakes if you left a bad Yelp review. I couldn't rule out Darlene, either, as greed and power exerted great influence over justifying abhorrent acts. She'd committed one crime for a dog; what else was she capable of? Joanna, I was inclined to give a pass, as I didn't want to think of Corky's "grandma" as a killer. But was I thinking objectively?

Okay, moving on to opportunity. Where had everybody been during the critical time frame? When

I'd been pulled away from my unlocked drug box by Fiona's impromptu leg gash?

Trudy had been there early in the day, before the emergency with Fiona, and she told me she'd left shortly after her encounter with Mrs. B. But had she really? Had the police checked her alibi for the time during which my drug box was unattended?

How about Martin Billings? Now that I thought about it, I believe he'd also had his altercation with Mrs. B before I'd left the unlocked drug box to attend to Fiona. But he, likewise, could have still been hanging around. And Darlene? Had the Chihuahua competition been before or after the Fiona fiasco? I couldn't remember, and my head started to hurt.

I knew Joanna had come in later in the day. Hadn't I already discovered and relocked my box before then?

The more I analyzed, the more tangled everything got. As tempting as it was to call Officer Lang and ask him to check Trudy's and Martin's whereabouts after their encounters with the victim, I managed to restrain myself. Barely. I only wish I knew where the police stood with the investigation.

Then there was the question as to whether someone else killed Mrs. Blankenship. Someone I'd overlooked, like Delores the groomer, for example. She'd had a slight tiff with the victim, not exactly a screaming match, but enough to take notice of. I hadn't mentioned her to the police. Did they even know about her?

I tossed my pen aside. "Okay, guys and gals, we need some fresh air and exercise, and maybe a break from this whole murder thing." Sierra perked up instantly, tail thudding against the floor like a bass drum. I rose from the table and retrieved her leash, which set her to running in excited circles, her claws clicking across the hardwood floor like a tap dancer on espresso. I grabbed her leash from the hook by the door. Evie blinked slowly from the dog bed, as though wondering what all the fuss was about, and Corky gave a half snore from the purse he'd practically lived in since I got him. Except I had one little problem. I only had one leash. Evie's leash had vanished sometime after the murder. And little Corky had remained collarless and leashless since I acquired him. What a negligent dog mom I was.

"Okay, change of plans," I announced to the canine trio. "We're going to the pet store."

Sierra barked her approval. Evie continued to blink at me with her large eyes. She'd probably never been in a pet store in her doggy life, which in human years probably amounted to thirty. Time to indoctrinate her into a whole new world.

If I couldn't solve a murder today, at least I could buy some overpriced dog accessories. In truth, I probably had a dozen discarded leashes and collars at the clinic. But I didn't want my new babies wearing some other dogs' hand-me-downs, particularly if the hand-me-downs had come from pets that had been put to sleep. Owners often left these items with me, as they didn't want them around to remind them of their beloved, deceased pet. Maybe I would also pick up some dog treats and toys. Besides, who knew whom I might run into that I could question? Amateur detectives always looked for clues wherever they found them.

I collected all three dogs, snapping Sierra's leash to her collar, slinging my bag with Corky inside over my shoulder, and tucking Evie under my arm. I drove to the Pet Super Center on the other side of town, our local emporium of pet paraphernalia and questionable customer fashion choices. I always marveled at the fact that the place managed to stay in business in a small community in which Starbucks had gone under.

Sierra's tail wagged furiously at the adventure, as she pressed her nose against the passenger window, leaving streaky nose art for me to clean later. Evie seemed content to curl into a ball on the front seat, unimpressed with the scenery, while Corky napped in my bag.

After arriving at the store, I grabbed a buggy and deposited Evie and my purse containing Corky in the "child" seat. Sierra walked obediently by the side of the cart, her tail still swishing, while Evie took in the surroundings with a detached eye that said pet stores were clearly beneath her. Inside, the store buzzed with activity as a crowd of people with their pets roamed the aisles looking for that "must-have" item. Dogs barked, cats hissed, and a parrot yelled, "Help!" from somewhere in the back. I hoped the bird didn't mean the word literally.

Rather proud that Sierra didn't bark or yank on her leash to sniff the butts of other dogs, I headed to the leash section. Evie regarded the other unruly dogs in the store with disdain reserved for royalty. As I rounded the corner to the aisle I wanted, I spied none other than Martin Billings, fingering a pronged choke collar. I took a quick step back, but not fast enough.

He spotted me behind the display of grooming shampoos. "Dr. Dixon," he called out, his voice like a megaphone. He walked toward me with the thick, menacing-looking collar in his hand, eyeing my neck as though imagining it encircling me like a choker necklace. "What a coincidence. Are you here to accuse me of murder again? Or just picking out something nice for yourself?"

Heat flooded my cheeks as the conversation within a thirty-foot radius paused. Several people turned to look. "I never accused you of anything, Mr. Billings." I lifted my chin. "I simply asked about your dog training services."

He gazed at Sierra, sitting quietly like a saint amidst the bedlam of the other animals, taking in the exchange with her curious eyes. "That's odd. Your dog appears to be quite well trained."

"Well, she is. Usually. But sometimes she . . ." Sometimes what? "She gets distracted easily."

He let out a hmmph of disbelief. "Looks attentive to me."

"Yes, well . . . I've decided against more training, thank you. Excuse me." I brushed past him, my heart thumping against my ribs. I could feel his glare burning into my back.

"The police came to talk to me," he continued. "Did you sic the cops on me?"

I spun on my heel to face him, painfully aware of the scene he was making, and my face blazed hotter.

Before I could answer, another familiar face emerged from the crowd. "Don't be so paranoid, Marty. The police are talking to everyone who attended the dog show. They even talked to me."

Delores. Come to my rescue again.

"It just feels personal." He ignored her, his eyes boring into mine. "People don't like being treated like suspects."

Didn't I know it!

Delores parked herself between me and the big man. "Why don't you leave the doc alone and go manhandle a squeaky toy? Work off some of that aggression."

He sneered at her, but walked away without another word, much to my relief. The onlookers began to disperse.

She turned to me as though nothing had happened. Apparently, nothing fazed the woman. "Good to see you again, Doc. You okay?"

"I am now." I let out a breath. "Thanks for jumping in. It seems like you're always rescuing me from nasty-tempered people."

"I don't like bullies." She bent and scratched Sierra's ears. "What a nice dog." Then she spied Evie. "Isn't that Evangelina Rose?"

"Yes. I found her huddled behind a crate after the paramedics took Mrs. Blankenship away. I didn't know what to do with her, so I took her home with me."

She let out a bark of laughter. "I'll bet the old Battleship is rolling over in her grave."

I laughed. "I hadn't thought of that, but you're probably right." I stroked Evie's fuzzy, erect ears. "But you know what? I think Evie likes her retirement."

"Evie?" Delores hooted. "Oh, wouldn't Mildred die if she heard you call her precious Evangelina Rose Evie. Assuming she wasn't already dead, of course."

I sobered. "Did the police really talk to you?"

"They did. But unlike *some* people who may have something to hide, it didn't upset me. They're just doing their job. Did they question you, too?"

"Yes." I didn't elaborate on how thoroughly.

She clucked her tongue. "Don't get me wrong. It's not as though I've never entertained the fantasy of ramming my grooming shears into Mildred's black heart. Theoretically speaking, of course. But a death, even one so well-deserved, is always tragic under such horrible circumstances."

"True. I performed CPR on her forever until the paramedics arrived." I shuddered, remembering the panic and frustration of not being able to restore a pulse.

"I'm surprised the fairgrounds doesn't have a defibrillator." Delores shook her head. "Seems like a lawsuit waiting to happen."

A defibrillator hadn't crossed my mind. I felt chagrined that as a health-care provider, I'd neglected to ask if one was available.

"Although I doubt anyone will sue over Mildred's death," she continued. "The old biddy didn't have any family. At least none that I know of, and I've known her for years."

"How sad." Maybe that explained why she was so . . . not nice. She had nobody but her dogs. "What happened to her husband?"

Delores shrugged. "Beats me. I never met him."

"What did the police ask you?"

"Oh, the usual. Where was I? Did I see anything? Did I know of anyone who might want to harm Mildred?" She rolled her eyes. "I almost told them who *didn't* want to harm her? They'd have to consider half the town as suspects."

"*Did* you see anything suspicious?" My hopes rose.

She shook her head. "No. I barely left my grooming booth all day. The only time I saw Mildred was when she was berating you. Besides, what possible reason would I have for killing her? If I went around murdering all the people who got under my skin, I'd have bodies stacked up in the back yard."

My hopes deflated. "What a nightmare. I hope they catch the killer soon."

She narrowed her eyes. "I wouldn't put it past Marty. He's a time bomb waiting to explode. I never did like that man."

"Then why would Mildred hire him to train and show her dogs?"

"No idea. She was a strange bird. Maybe she liked her dogs trained with the same love and gentleness as a boot camp sergeant." She gave Evie a pat on the head and checked her watch. "Well, I better skedaddle. I've got a bunch of errands to run and a schnauzer to shave."

"Nice to see you again. And thanks again for stopping that scene with Martin."

"Anytime. Next time, just throw a leash on him." She gave me a sardonic wink and disappeared down the aisle, leaving me to untangle my nerves after the Billings showdown—and to process Delores' unexpected heroics.

After becoming the unwilling star of the pet store's impromptu CSI drama, I wanted nothing more than to get out of there as soon as possible. I hurried back to the leash aisle and measured Corky's tiny neck, mentally adding "escape artist," then opted for a cat harness instead of a collar. Scratch that. Make it a kitten harness. I bought Evie a leash to match her blingy rhinestone-studded diva collar, and hustled to the cash register, bypassing the treats and toys, ignoring the stares and whispers from other customers.

Outside, the summer heat hit me like the breath of something lurking—thick, oppressive, and sinister, as though evil waited just out of sight. What if I encountered Martin Billings again, like in a dark alley, and Delores wasn't around to protect me? Officer Lang's words echoed in my head. *You've rattled somebody's cage.* I began to regret my efforts to help the police find the killer. Maybe I needed to invest in some grooming shears.

As I opened my car door and set Evie and Corky in the front seat, someone called my name. I turned to find Trudy approaching, and my stomach lurched. Was *everyone* who was at that dog show last week patronizing the pet store?

Plastering on a smile, I said, "Hi, Trudy. How are you?"

Her brow wrinkled. "The police came by my apartment this morning asking about the murder."

My pulse skipped. "Oh?"

"Yes. I just wondered how they knew I was there. Did you tell them?" She gave me a wounded look that hit me like a sucker punch, and I suddenly felt like a Judas Iscariot with dog treats.

"Why would I tell them?" It wasn't exactly a lie, not that I hadn't broken the ninth commandment repeatedly during the past few days. I needed to deflect suspicion away from myself. "They're questioning a lot of people, even me. It's just routine."

Her confusion deepened, like she was assembling a puzzle, and I was the one shady missing piece. "I still don't understand. It wasn't until after I saw you yesterday that they showed up. Who else would have told them I was there?"

"They have ways of finding these things out." I forced a casual shrug. "A lot of people could have seen you. This *is* a small town."

I watched the wheels turning in her mind. Silence stretched between us, thick enough to choke on.

Time to change the subject. "How's Bentley?"

She brought her eyes back to mine, as though her thoughts still lingered miles away. "Oh, he's fine. Thank you for asking."

"Well, I've got to be going. Good to see you. Let me know if you need any help with Bentley." I scurried to the driver's side and jumped in, giving Trudy a cheery wave before speeding off. In my rearview mirror, I could see her standing in the same spot, bewilderment on her face.

"That was awkward," I muttered to the dogs, who paid me no attention. After the scary encounter with Billings, I didn't need another weird run-in. And Trudy's not-quite accusation left my insides twisting into knots. Did she believe me when I indirectly denied being the one to enlighten the police about her? I couldn't be sure. I suppose if I thought someone had ratted me out, I would feel betrayed, too.

I'd rattled too many cages. Time to go back to being a mild-mannered veterinarian and leave crime solving to the paid professional crime fighters.

Chapter Twenty-Three

Once I'd made it home, I was no longer in the mood to walk the dogs. All I wanted to do was lock myself in the house, pull down the shades, and curl up in the fetal position in my bed. For the rest of my life. Or until the police caught the killer.

But Sierra insisted I keep my promise. She bounced up and down, woofing softly in my face until I caved in.

"Fine, you win," I grumbled. "But if I run into another murder suspect, that's it. I'll need all three of you for emotional support animals."

I fitted Corky's new harness on him and clipped Evie's new leash to her collar, then set out, determined to keep to the shady side of the street despite Sierra spotting the flock of pigeons pecking on breadcrumbs on the sunny side of the road. Her entire body went rigid as she lunged, leash taut, ready to bolt across the street and liberate the sidewalk from its feathered invaders. And Billings accused me of lying about Sierra's distractibility.

Reining her in, I attempted to work out a rhythm

with the three dogs between Sierra's pulling, Evie's wee legs trotting as fast as she could to keep up, and Corky plopping mournfully on the sidewalk as if the leash and harness were a cruel joke and the sidewalk a battlefield he never enlisted for. How quickly I'd forgotten puppy leash training.

I walked backward, cooing baby talk to him like a deranged nanny, trying to coax Corky into taking even one brave step forward. "Come on, buddy! Who's a big boy? You can do it!" I chirped, clapping my hands like an over-caffeinated preschool teacher. Corky stared at me, utterly unimpressed, then let out a dramatic sigh and flopped onto his side like he'd just completed a triathlon. Meanwhile, Evie zipped in frantic little circles, her rhinestone leash tangling around my ankles like decorative bondage, and Sierra continued to lunge for the pigeons, threatening the integrity of the ligaments holding together my shoulder joint.

My backward shuffle turned into a sideways stumble as I tried to untwist myself without dropping a leash—or my dignity. A passing jogger gave us a wide berth, probably not wanting to become an unwilling participant in our bizarre bondage. Corky finally lifted his head, yawned, and gave me a look that said, *You're going to have to carry me, peasant.* I was beginning to think he had a point.

I sighed and scooped him up. It had been a mistake to bring him with the other two dogs. Gingerly stepping out of the tethers wrapping around my ankles, I gave Sierra's leash a firm tug and said, "No!" She gave me a look—part frustration that I'd interrupted her vital mission, and part, *Sorry, Mom, I got carried away.*

"We are going to walk properly," I declared. Once

Corky's participation was no longer required, Evie and Sierra fell into step beside me, their mismatched strides surprisingly in sync despite the glaring differences in their legs. We circled the block without further mishap and returned to the house.

Much to my delight, Nick phoned later that evening, just as I was cleaning up a Corky puddle in the kitchen. I filled him in on my adventures at the pet store.

"I'm worried, Amy. Billings is unhinged, and Trudy sounds a bit strange. Plus, what with Darlene breaking into your house pleading insanity, this whole thing is getting out of hand and way too personal."

I flopped on the couch, landing on a squeaky toy that squawked beneath me. "Need I remind you it was *your* idea to question these people like a pair of small-town Sherlock Holmes?" I fished the toy out from under my behind.

"Yeah, I know, but I didn't want the police to just slap the cuffs on you and call it a day. You know how they think they've wrapped up the case, so they don't bother to investigate any further. At least on TV. An innocent person stands condemned until an outside party proves their innocence."

"As Officer Lang reminded me, we're not in an episode of *Hallmark Movies and Mysteries*." Except I wouldn't mind settling for the romantic wrap-up at the end.

Nick sighed. "Plus, I didn't think anyone would catch on to what we were doing. We were just chatting about the murder like the rest of the people in town."

Evie jumped up and nestled against me. I scratched her ears. "Well, no one's actually threatened me. But

I'm done playing Nancy Drew. I'm sticking to neutering dogs and dispensing flea medication."

"I just want you to be careful."

I didn't say what I was thinking—that it might already be too late for careful. But I promised him I'd be careful before hanging up. Then I promptly tripped over Corky on the way to the bathroom.

The next morning, I slipped into my Sunday school class early, just in case the Sunday school director decided to boot me from preschool teacher duty due to my being a murder suspect. If I had to leave in disgrace, I didn't want to be marched out in front of a group of wide-eyed four and five-year-olds who might need therapy later. But to my relief, no one approached me and asked me to resign. That might have had something to do with the fact that recruiting preschool Sunday school teachers was usually met with the same resistance as one uses to fend off door-to-door aluminum siding salesmen. So maybe they figured I could continue teaching at least until the police dragged me away in handcuffs.

With the few quiet minutes to myself, I sank into the only adult-sized chair in the room—my sacred throne—and bowed my head. *Lord, I don't know how I managed to get myself into this mess, but I'd sure appreciate it if You could get me out of it. Preferably before I end up on the evening news as either a felony suspect or a homicide victim.* A sense of guilt enveloped me, as this wasn't the first time I'd prayed that prayer. In my mind's eye, I could envision my

Heavenly Father, arms crossed, giving me the world's most patient but exasperated look. *Again, Amy?* He would say. *Did you bother to consult Me before taking matters into your own hands?*

Yeah . . . about that.

If I were being honest—and since I was praying, honesty seemed advisable—I hadn't exactly consulted God before running amok on my wild detective goose chase, which had sounded like such a good idea at the time. Never mind that a large part of my motivation involved spending more time with Nick, who I was fairly certain was a divine gift with a wicked smile wrapped in a red vendor's apron.

I tried to justify my actions to the Good Lord by shifting the blame to the police, explaining to Him that they had all but locked me in the slammer. They'd scared all rational thought clean out of my brain, forcing me to conduct my own investigation. But I had the feeling that not only did God already know what had happened, but He wasn't buying my half-baked defense. The truth was, the only investigating I should have been doing was into my own prayer life. Some role model for impressionable preschoolers.

My heartfelt moment of self-recrimination ended with a bang—literally—when Peyton barreled into the room like a pint-sized hurricane, her Mary Janes clacking loudly on the tile floor.

"Miss Amy, they gots doughnuts in the fellowship hall!" she announced breathlessly, arms waving like a windmill.

I took in the chocolate icing smeared on her hands, face, and even a suspicious streak in her curly, blonde hair. Fighting back a laugh, I said, "I see. Why don't we go into the bathroom and wash the frosting off your hands and face before it spreads to the furniture?" Or me.

"Don't need to." She grinned, showing a missing tooth in the front of her mouth. "I can just lick it." To prove her point, she bent her arm like a contortionist and proceeded to slurp chocolate off her wrist.

I made a mental note to pick up some wet wipes. Several more preschoolers trickled in, bringing with them a symphony of laughter, squeals, and jelly-stained enthusiasm. Within seconds, the room came alive with commotion, the pure, innocent kind that doesn't involve murder suspects and bad decisions.

I let the noise wash over me, pulling me from my tangled thoughts and back into my students' simpler world. Oh, to be young again, when the worst mess you made could be fixed with soap and water, and nobody expected you to solve a murder before snack time.

Later, the sermon buoyed my spirits, as Pastor Bob seemed to preach directly to me with Biblical examples of people who had messed up big time, but God still rescued them. He even used them for His glory, despite their failings. I drove home with a renewed sense of peace and determination to let the police and God handle the mess.

Nick called later in the afternoon, and I invited him to come over for the spaghetti dinner he'd missed. He didn't need much convincing. I had a pot of sauce simmering by the time he knocked on the door, sending a garlic-scented cloud throughout the house. Granted, the sauce came from a jar, but it still gave off a delicious aroma. Spaghetti noodles bubbled merrily on the next burner.

I wiped my hands on a dish towel and opened the door. Nick stood there, hands shoved in the pockets of his jeans, wearing a tight-fitting T-shirt and his crooked smile that said he was glad to be here. At the sight of him, my heart began flapping around in my chest like a trapped bird.

"Smells good," he said, stepping inside and inhaling deeply. "Better than the peanut butter sandwich I had for lunch."

I laughed and closed the door behind him. "Stick with me, and you'll never have to suffer through sad sandwiches again." Oops. I'd just broken the ninth commandment again. If things progressed between us, the way I hoped, at some point, the man would figure out that spaghetti was pretty much my one and only specialty.

He grinned again, and for a moment, the heaviness of the past few days lifted. He followed me into the kitchen, where the table was already set and two glasses of iced tea sweated on coasters. Evie lounged in the dog bed, eyeing Nick with the solemn suspicion of a tiny security guard. Sierra wagged her tail so hard that she was in danger of knocking over a chair. Corky let out an adorable yap and jumped up and down in an effort to attract Nick's attention.

Nick crouched and scratched Sierra behind the ears with one hand while rubbing Corky's exposed, squirming belly with the other. "With the exception of Evie, I seem to have a fan club." He looked up at me. "Need any help?"

"No, you're busy. Besides, everything's ready. Have a seat." I pulled a loaf of garlic bread from the oven with the flourish of someone unveiling a masterpiece. Again, store bought, but smelling delicious.

He slid into my kitchen chair like he belonged there, while Sierra and Corky continued to make nuisances of themselves, and watched while I strained the noodles and plopped them into a serving bowl. After I dished up the sauce and placed it on the table, I took the seat across from him. He reached for my hand, said a short prayer, and unfolded his napkin. Paper napkin, but at least I'd folded it.

"Sierra! Corky! Quit showing off!" I scolded. Sierra gave me a canine sigh, but obediently headed to her bed, curling in beside Evie. Corky continued to pogo stick beside Nick. His cuteness covered a multitude of doggy sins, so I didn't fuss at him.

"This looks great. I'm starved." Nick helped himself to a heaping mound of spaghetti and covered it in store-bought sauce. He took a bite. "Mmm. This is really good, Amy."

"Thanks." I basked in his praise as I tried to eat my spaghetti like a civilized adult without slurping up the noodles. I'd never mastered the art of winding pasta around a fork, so every bite was a gamble.

For a moment, there was only the clinking of forks and the low hum of the air conditioner battling the heat outside. It felt surprisingly normal, considering I was still technically under a murder cloud. I kept waiting for Nick to bring up the subject of the elephant in the room, for the easygoing dinner to shift into another round of *Let's talk about the murder*. But he didn't.

I caught myself sneaking peeks at Nick, warmth unfurling through my chest like a blooming flower, unable to keep a smile from spreading across my face.

Maybe, just maybe, everything wasn't as doomed as it felt. Eating spaghetti with Nick was something I could allow myself to get used to.

We lingered over dinner longer than necessary, picking at second helpings and letting the conversation meander from silly stories to small-town gossip. I had just finished recounting a disastrous vacation Bible school craft project involving glue sticks, glitter, and a distracted teenage volunteer when Nick finally leaned back in his chair, his expression turning serious. My stomach tightened a little.

"So," he said casually, although his eyes said otherwise, "anything strange happen today?"

There it was. I dropped my gaze to my plate, suddenly fascinated by a lone meatball hanging out near the edge.

"No, thank goodness," I said, stabbing the meatball for emphasis. "Like I said yesterday, from now on, I'm leaving the murder stuff to the professionals."

He reached across the table, brushing his fingers lightly over mine. Just a small touch, but enough to send a ridiculous jolt of comfort—and something else—up my arm.

"Good. I feel responsible for putting you in harm's way."

I busied myself brushing nonexistent crumbs off the table. "You were just trying to help. Who knew things would get so weird?" I grinned. "Besides, despite everything, I had a really good time with you this week."

He smiled back, and the room felt lighter. "Yeah, me too."

After we cleared the plates and loaded the

dishwasher, which somehow felt like playing house—another ritual I could get used to—we ended up on the couch, a respectable gap between us that still buzzed with unspoken energy.

"Do you want to try for another movie? I promise I'll make a valiant attempt to stay awake this time."

"Sure." He grinned. "But only if you have popcorn."

"You're in luck." I hopped up, glad I had a box of microwave popcorn in the pantry. "You pick the movie." I stuck the bag of popcorn in the microwave, then poked my head around the corner. "Nothing where anyone dies."

To my delight, he chose a rom-com, which I found appropriately fitting considering our past week's adventures. I also knew that most guys would prefer action and machismo over chick-flicks, so I appreciated his effort to take my mind off crime scenes, interrogation rooms, and murder suspects.

We munched on popcorn and laughed at the silly twists and turns the plotline took until the climax, when, of course, the guy and the girl realize they've fallen for each other and live happily ever after. For a few moments, as the credits rolled, the air between us felt charged. I became suddenly hyperaware of how close Nick was, the faint scent of his aftershave lingering between us, fresh and woodsy.

I jumped up to take the popcorn bowl and glasses to the kitchen. He trailed after me more slowly.

"I'd better go." His voice held a huskiness that sent my pulse thrumming in my ears. "Thanks for dinner."

"Anytime," I said, somehow forgetting every single cool, casual thing I had ever planned to say to a yummy man standing in my kitchen.

He lingered for half a second longer, as if considering something. And then, with a little smile that curled at the corners of his mouth like he knew *exactly* what he was doing, he reached out and tapped the tip of my nose with his finger. A tinge of disappointment fluttered through my heart, wishing his finger had dropped down an inch or so, followed by his lips. "Stay out of trouble, Amy."

"Define 'trouble,'" I said, grinning up at him.

He laughed and shook his head as he moved toward the door. "If you have to ask, you're already halfway there."

I walked him to the door, then leaned against the doorframe, watching him disappear into the night, feeling a little like the heroine of a rom-com where the credits were about to roll—except, of course, in my movie, there was still a murder to solve and about ninety-seven ways to get myself into even deeper trouble.

Still, for tonight, it was enough.

I closed the door, locked it, and turned around just in time for Evie to give me the same exasperated look I'd imagined God giving me earlier.

"Don't start," I told her.

But even as I spoke, I was smiling.

Chapter Twenty-Four

I let the dogs out for one last romp, gave them their goodnight treats, and was halfway through wiping down the kitchen counters when I spied Nick's cell phone on the table, sitting there like a lost puppy.

Great. It suddenly occurred to me that I didn't know where he lived, so I couldn't hop in the truck and deliver it to him. *Note to self: get Nick's address.* I figured he'd notice soon enough. Phones were basically life support these days, right? Surely, he'd realize he was missing a vital piece of himself and come back.

Just in case he returned, I stayed dressed. I didn't want to be caught off-guard in my ratty nightshirt with a washed, unadorned face. I busied myself by cleaning things that were already clean and straightening things that were already straight. By the time the clock ticked past eleven—way past my bedtime—reality set in. Either Nick hadn't missed his phone, or he had a higher tolerance for being phoneless than the average human.

I changed into my nightshirt, washed my face, and stuck his phone in my purse to take to the clinic in the morning. Then I crawled into bed, musing on how nice and normal the day had been, replaying the evening in my head, a smile tugging on my lips.

Normal with Nick felt good. Granted, our paths might never have crossed if not for an unplanned stint as the dog show veterinarian, an unexpected murder, and our clumsy attempts to play detective. But after the rollercoaster of the past week, exhaustion pressed down on me—not just physically, but in that deep, bone-heavy way that comes from living too long under a shadow of stress. I just wanted my life back.

Funny, I used to think running a veterinary clinic was high-stress, what with juggling late-night emergencies, finicky cat owners, and the occasional hysterical hamster parent. Not to mention trying to pay the bills when people thought I had some nerve charging for my services when I was supposed to "love animals." If only they knew how much it cost to operate a clinic. Still, all those frustrations paled in comparison to getting tangled up in a homicide.

As I stared at the ceiling, unable to sleep, my thoughts traced the seemingly innocent chain of events that had landed me in this predicament, starting with one small favor. Helping out a colleague. Trying to do the right thing.

What had I learned from this experience?

Maybe, when Dr. Collins' frantic wife called, I should have said, "Sorry, I'm busy" without feeling guilty. Maybe, in the future, I should stop volunteering for jobs that might involve dead bodies.

No, that wasn't me. Despite everything that had happened, if I had it to do all over again, I would—with the exception of making sure my controlled drug box was locked. Helping people, even when it came at a cost, was just part of who I was. Even if it came with unexpected turmoil.

I had finally drifted off to sleep when the unwelcome intrusion of my cell phone butted into what had started out to be a great dream in which Nick's sweet little nose tap had led to something much steamier. Ripped out of REM bliss, I groped blindly for the phone. For one brief, bleary-eyed moment, I thought it might be Nick himself, calling to ask about his missing phone. Then my brain, slow but not completely useless, reminded me that he couldn't exactly do that without his phone.

"Hello?" I murmured, praying it was a wrong number or a robocall telling me my car warranty had expired. Anything but an emergency requiring me to haul my weary body out of bed and down to the clinic in the wee hours of the morning. Yes, I could always refer them to the emergency clinic, but whenever possible, I wanted to be there for my clients. As I said, helping people, even when it came with a cost, was just who I was. Often, simply talking to someone or offering some easy suggestions was enough to take care of the problem and ease the owner's mind.

"Amy? This is Trudy." Her voice verged on hysteria, and I instantly went on wide-awake alert.

"Trudy, what's wrong?"

"It's Bentley. He's been having a seizure for five minutes now, and it won't stop."

I mentally kicked myself for not sending her home with some rectal valium to administer in an emergency such as this. My forgetfulness this week was coming back to bite me big time. I could send them to the emergency clinic, but my clinic was much closer to where she lived, and time was of the essence with an ongoing seizure. If I could get him stabilized, Trudy could transfer him to the emergency clinic for overnight monitoring. It shouldn't take long, and with any luck, I'd be back in my bed within the hour.

"I'm so sorry to call you at this time of night, but I didn't know what else to do."

"It's okay, you did the right thing. Meet me at the clinic." I switched on the bedside lamp, then jumped out of bed, pulling on my jeans. My nightshirt got tucked in somewhere along the way. It was neither cute nor coordinated, but it was fast.

"O . . . okay, thank you." Her words caught on a sob.

I disconnected and slid my feet into my flip-flops. I didn't waste time combing my hair. Racing through the house, I snatched my purse and my keys from the kitchen counter. When I got to the door, Sierra stood wagging her tail, a hopeful expression on her face. She loved going to the clinic after hours with me, and, to be honest, somewhere in the back of my mind, I felt safer having her with me. Not that any dog ever rescued anyone from danger by licking their assailant's face to death. But still . . .

To my surprise, Evie, likewise, had left her comfy nest, standing guard at the door and staring up at me with those enormous eyes like she, too, had a stethoscope and a license to practice.

"Fine, you both can come." I reached down to pick up Evie when Corky came bounding over, determined not to be left behind, his less-than-perfect tail twirling in circles. Sighing, I stuffed him into my purse, tucked Evie under my arm, and let Sierra run free to the truck.

Sierra jumped in the moment I opened the truck door. I set Evie and Corky on the seat, thrust the key into the ignition, and backed out of the driveway with the practiced ease of someone who had done this maneuver a few times in her pajamas.

Fortunately, my clinic was only a few blocks from my house, a factor that had figured prominently into deciding on its location. I had spent too many hours driving to and from various clinics I'd worked for in the past, and knew I wanted to live close to my work. Hardly any traffic traveled the roads this late, and no stop lights impeded me on my mission to stop Bentley's seizure.

I pulled into the parking lot, which was well lit by a single street lamp, and extracted the animals. After unlocking the door, leaving it open for Trudy, I turned off the burglar alarm and flipped on the lights.

"Sierra, office," I said unnecessarily, as she was already heading for her bed away from home. I took Corky out of my purse and settled him and Evie into the dog bed. Corky immediately climbed out, apparently having gotten a second wind, and launched an attack on the leg of my chair.

"No, Corky." I redirected his attention to a chew toy, hoping he would get the message. "Chew the giraffe, not my chair."

But I didn't have time to worry about gnawed chair legs, as the buzzer to the outside door sounded. "Come on in," I called, stepping out of the office. Trudy stood in the doorway, her crate in her hand.

"Bring him into the first exam room," I said, motioning her in.

She made no attempt to follow me. "The seizure

seems to have stopped on its own."

"That's good. But let me have a look at him, anyway, since you're here."

She moved slowly, then lingered by the exam room door, an odd look on her face like I might whack her with a bill the moment she stepped inside. Relieved that the life-and-death emergency had passed, I was still puzzled over her reluctance to have me check her dog. Did she think I wouldn't charge her if I didn't examine Bentley now that they were here? Sorry, lady, once I'm rousted out of bed and stuffed a wiggling puppy in my purse, the meter is running, whether the seizure has stopped or not.

I crossed the room and took the crate from her hands. Something was off. It felt suspiciously light. Like suspiciously suspicious. Granted, Bentley was small, but the crate shouldn't feel this weightless. I placed it on the table and peered inside. No dog.

"Uh, Trudy," I said, straightening slowly, "where's Bentley?"

To my horror, I found myself staring down the barrel of a gun, small, shiny, and shaking in her hand like a Chihuahua on Red Bull.

I froze, and my brain did that thing where it tried to detach from my body and pretend this was happening to someone else. But it wasn't. The blood drained from my extremities, rendering them like rubber.

"Trudy, what are you doing?" I took a step back on wobbly legs I feared wouldn't support me.

"I know you suspected me." Her voice wavered, but her grip didn't. "That's why you told the police about me."

I shook my head. "No, I *know* you didn't kill Mrs.

Blankenship," I said, trying to sound calm and not like a woman picturing her own obituary headline. "You weren't even there. You told me yourself that you left right after you talked to her, remember?"

"I *said* I left. But I didn't." She edged closer, and I edged backward until my spine bumped against the hard wall. I instinctively pressed myself flatter, as if I could Houdini myself through the Sheetrock.

"Wha . . . what do you mean?"

"I didn't leave. I was too upset to drive home, so I wandered around the fairgrounds trying to calm down."

I nodded like that was a totally normal thing to do after a meltdown at a dog show. "O . . . kay."

"I ended up near the Jack Russell ring. That's when I saw you with that woman, the one who had the dog with seizures."

I swallowed against the dryness of my throat. "Yes, I remember. The Cocker spaniel."

"I watched you open your box. You gave her some phenobarbital for her dog."

"Yes," I whispered. "What does that have to do with . . ." I suddenly knew where this was going.

"Then you got called away. Your drug box was just sitting there, open." Her voice cracked. "And I thought, 'I wonder how Mildred Blankenship would like to live like Bentley? Doped up. Helpless.' Maybe then she'd understand how I felt." Trudy's eyes shimmered with manic tears. "I didn't intend to kill her, you've got to believe me."

"I do," I said. *Sort of. The crazy kind of belief.*

"I only meant to give her a few pills. Just enough to make her drowsy. Make her miss her competition. And . . . and maybe people would think she had a drug problem or something."

I didn't tell Trudy that Mrs. B had already shown Evie and taken first place before Trudy drugged her. That information probably wouldn't help.

"But then, I don't know what happened. I just dumped the whole bottle into my hand." She let out a shaky breath and shook her head, as though half disbelief and half regret. "You don't understand how it was. I was so angry at the way she completely blew me off about Bentley. She didn't care."

I held up my hands, as though that would deflect a bullet. "I do understand. Mrs. Blankenship was a horrible woman. She should have worked with you to come up with a mutually beneficial solution. But lots of people have epileptic dogs. It's not the end of the world."

"She promised me I could make a lot of money by breeding him." Trudy's voice broke. "If I just wanted a pet, I could have gone to the dog pound."

I didn't think pointing out that there were no guarantees in life would help. Nor was this the time to advocate for adopting a pet from a shelter. I needed her to believe I was on her side.

"What she did was wrong." My eyes darted frantically for anything I might use as a weapon. Clipboard? Syringe? Cotton balls? Not likely to help in this confined space.

She ignored my comment. "And then *you* lied to me." Trudy locked eyes with me, tears streaming down her face. "I only came here asking for a second opinion to see what you knew. You told me you didn't know what killed Mildred when it was *your* phenobarbital. That's when I knew you suspected me."

Although I knew trying to reason with her probably wouldn't work, I had to try. "No, that's not true. I didn't want people to know where the drug came from because it looked bad for me."

"And then you told the police about me."

Guilty. But what was one more lie at this point? "Why would you think that?" I tried to make my voice sound as convincing as possible.

"Because they came to my house the next morning after I was here. How else would they have known I was at the dog show?"

"Like I told you yesterday, they talked to a lot of people. Anyone could have seen you there."

Her accusing eyes filmed over with sadness. "How would you like to have to live your whole life on phenobarbital, never knowing when another seizure will come?"

"There are worse things, Trudy, believe me. Bentley isn't suffering."

"I didn't plan to kill her," she repeated.

"I know, Trudy. Just let me help you. The police will take everything into consideration."

She stared at the wall that was holding me up, silent for a moment. Then she said, "It's too late." Keeping her eyes on me, she pulled a piece of paper from her pocket and laid it on the exam table. "Sign that."

I glanced at the paper, but didn't pick it up. "What is it?"

"It's a confession saying that you killed Mrs. Blankenship."

My stomach did a nosedive. "But . . . but I didn't."

"You're going to confess to her murder. Then

you're going to feel so remorseful that you're going to commit suicide."

Insanity shone out from her eyes. My throat closed with fear, and my heart banged so hard against my ribs I was afraid they'd break. I supposed a few broken ribs didn't matter if I was dead.

"What?" I squeaked. "I'm not going to shoot myself, Trudy."

"No," she said, disturbingly calm now. "You're going to take phenobarbital, just like Mildred. Poetic justice and all."

Think, Amy. Think! "I, uh . . . I don't have any. I haven't gotten around to ordering more."

Her eyes narrowed. "I don't believe you."

My pulse thrummed in my ears so loudly I could barely hear her. "It's true. I'm out. I've had to write prescriptions all week."

"Let me see. Show me your controlled drugs." She waved the gun toward the hallway. When I didn't move, she added, *"Now."*

Great. Now she'd have proof I lied. I left the security of the wall, my brain scrambling for a way to escape. But she jabbed her gun in my back and marched me into the surgery, where my controlled drug box hung on the wall. If I tried to wrench free, I'd likely end up with a bullet in my back. But if I didn't come up with something fast, I would end up face-down in my own clinic, framed for a murder I didn't commit, overdosed on my own inventory, with Corky chewing up my flip-flops post-mortem.

Maybe if I told her I didn't have the key . . . No, then she'd just shoot me for sure. I could tell she was close to her breaking point.

"Open it."

I hesitated just long enough to get a jab in the spine with cold steel.

"I don't want to shoot you, but I will if I have to."

Great. A reluctant murderer with a trigger finger. If only I had a panic button installed somewhere in the clinic. And, assuming I did, if only I could get to it with a loaded gun jammed in my back. But I didn't and I couldn't, so I dug the keys from my jeans and inserted the key into the lock of the controlled drug cabinet. The fleeting thought ran through my mind that I should have just sent her to the emergency clinic. This is what I got for trying to help someone, yet again.

The door to the cabinet clicked open, and Trudy reached around me to pluck a new, unopened bottle of 1.5-grain phenobarbital off the shelf.

"You lied to me again." Disappointment colored her tone.

"Sorry, but I have this intense desire to live."

Nick's face flashed through my mind. Sorrow washed over me that I might never have the chance to explore our relationship further. I didn't even get a first—or last—kiss from him.

She shoved the gun into me again and spun me around, holding the pill bottle in one hand like a coveted prize and the weapon with the other.

"Now walk over to the sink and get a glass of water."

"Trudy, think about what you're doing." I stalled. "Nobody will believe I killed Mildred. I had no motive. And nobody will believe I committed suicide either. I'm not the type."

"Shut up!" Her voice rose with desperation. "Go

back into that room and sign that paper. Then swallow those pills."

Out of ideas, I shuffled toward the room, my brain blank. If only I could somehow distract her and wrestle the gun away from her. But how? Throw the glass of water in her face? Launch myself backward into her, throwing her off balance? Thrust a blind elbow behind me into her gut? But all of those options could end up getting me shot.

Please, God, I need a miracle.

Before I knew what was happening, I heard an unholy screech like nothing I'd ever heard before. A snarling, high-pitched screech.

Evie.

She tore out of the office like a four-pound fury and latched onto Trudy's ankle like a rabid piranha, demonic growls emanating from her throat. I twisted loose from Trudy's grip and stood transfixed by the sight, unable to move.

"Ow!" Trudy shrieked. "Get it off me!" She staggered backward, kicking her leg to dislodge the four-pound attack dog, but Evie held on like a snarling pit bull.

Trudy swung the gun wildly, and fear jolted me into action. I grabbed the nearest object I could find—the fire extinguisher—and clocked Trudy up the side of the head like my life depended on it. Because it did.

The gun went off. The bang echoed through the clinic, and Trudy crumpled to the floor like a marionette with cut strings—Evie still attached. The gun skittered across the floor, and I raced after it on legs that felt like Jell-O.

My shaking hand closed over the gun, slick with

sweat and adrenaline. Nausea rose in my throat. I stumbled to the drug cabinet, shoved the gun inside, and locked it.

I forced deep breaths into my lungs. My brain short-circuited. What now?

Trudy groaned and raised her head, one arm reaching for Evie.

"Oh, no you don't!" I kicked her reaching arm for good measure, although my flip-flop inflicted about as much damage as swatting a bear with a dish towel.

"You want to hurt me, fine. But you don't hurt my dog." I bent and pried Evie from her leg. "It's okay, sweetheart. That's enough. You got her."

Trudy's head flopped back to the floor with a dull thud.

Evie blinked once, her mouth bloody and tongue hanging out, panting. Then, right after gnawing on a killer, she showered my face with kisses. It was rather gross, and I hoped Trudy didn't carry any blood-borne diseases, but they were the best kisses I'd ever had. Which was a little sad, if I thought about it too hard—which got me to thinking about Nick's kisses, which I had yet to experience.

Speaking of whom . . . The man himself came running through the front door. "Amy? Are you all right? I thought I heard a gun—" He stopped. His face went white as his eyes scanned the scene: me cradling a bloodied, panting Evie, Trudy unconscious on the floor, bleeding from Chihuahua bites on her ankle, and a fire extinguisher with a dent like a murder weapon from *Clue*.

"What in the world?"

At the sight of him, the dam burst. "It was Trudy."

I threw myself against him and sobbed into his chest. "She killed Mildred and tried to kill me. Evie saved my life!"

Nick gently peeled me away from him, eyes wide. "We need to call the police. And tie her up."

I sniveled and dashed to the front office, returning with an armful of leashes. "Here. You do it. I can't tie good knots under pressure. Or, honestly, ever."

Nick did the honors while I picked up the landline with shaky hands and punched in 911.

As the dispatcher answered, I looked down at Evie, still perched on my hip like a bloodthirsty gremlin. "You," I whispered, "are getting steak for dinner."

Chapter Twenty-Five

The flashing red-and-blue lights painted the front windows like a '70s disco ball. I sat on the clinic floor, Evie curled in my lap, still buzzing with adrenaline. Sierra stood over me like a worried sentry who wasn't quite sure what had happened. Some guard dog. Corky continued to squeak his toy, oblivious to the entire drama. From now on, I was bringing Evie with me for protection.

A uniformed officer hovered over Trudy, now handcuffed and semi-conscious. Another officer stood at the reception desk, taking Nick's statement. I'd already given mine—twice, though the first time was mostly hyperventilating and sobbing. The paramedic had offered me oxygen. I declined. I had my own source of oxygen should I feel the need, and didn't want to pay a high insurance deductible for county oxygen.

Nick crossed the room, crouched beside me, and handed me a bottle of water. "You okay?"

"No," I said, voice croaky. "But I'm not dead, so that's a win."

He gave a half-smile. "You really clocked her."

"I think I sprained something." I flexed my wrist and winced. "Also, pretty sure I'm going to need therapy. Possibly for the rest of my life."

"Can't say I blame you."

We sat in silence for a moment. Then, "She wanted me to write a confession saying I killed Mrs. Blankenship," I said. "Then take the same drugs."

Nick's jaw clenched.

"She even had a suicide note prepared. Typed. With correct grammar and punctuation. She must have Grammarly on her computer. Honestly, I was impressed."

"That's one word for it."

Evie snorted in her sleep, her little tongue poking out between her teeth. At least her tongue didn't still have Trudy's blood on it.

I looked down at her and stroked her soft fur. "She saved my life," I said, for perhaps the twentieth time.

"I know. I wonder if she recognized Trudy as the one who killed her owner."

"Guess we'll never know."

I suddenly realized I didn't know why he was here. I'd just assumed he'd appeared from out of nowhere like the hero in the action movie.

"Uh, Nick, not that I'm complaining, but what made you think about rushing into the clinic at"—I consulted my watch—"one a.m.?"

"I forgot my phone, which I needed first thing in the morning. I was driving back to your place, hoping you'd still be awake, when I saw your truck in the parking lot." He ran a hand through his hair and gave me his crooked grin. "I thought I'd stop to see if you needed any help with a patient. I had no idea what I was walking into."

I returned the grin. "You can say that again."

"Then I heard the gunshot, and I just reacted." His expression turned serious. "I couldn't bear the thought that you could be hurt or . . ." His voice trailed off.

My almost hero. Tough to be beaten out by a four-pound Chihuahua. Still, Nick had run headlong into danger to rescue me.

I smiled, even as tears stung the corners of my eyes. "Thank you. For coming."

"Anytime." He nodded toward the officer leading Trudy out. "They'll take her to the hospital first. Get her checked out. Then jail."

"I hope I didn't injure Trudy too badly." I felt a prick of guilt, but only a tiny prick. "She really didn't mean to kill Mildred at first," I said quietly. "But she definitely meant to kill *me.*"

Nick reached over and gently tucked a strand of hair behind my ear. "You don't have to be fair to someone who held a gun to your back."

"I know." I leaned into his hand. "It's just—I keep wondering if I could have done something different."

He looked at me, eyes searching mine. "The only reason you're alive is because you stayed calm and kept thinking. And you have a four-pound psychopath with excellent timing."

I laughed softly. "I guess Billings' boot camp paid off."

Nick's hand lingered on my jaw. "You're amazing, you know that?"

I opened my mouth to object, but he didn't let me.

"No. You are. Brave. Smart. Kind. A little snarky.

And now you've got attempted murder on your résumé."

"Don't forget a head injury I gave someone with a fire extinguisher."

"Like I said. Amazing." His eyes held a hint of something that sent my adrenaline surge soaring again.

He brought his face close. My breath caught.

I tilted my chin up just slightly. "You know," I murmured, "this is probably not the *best* moment for a kiss."

Nick leaned closer. "True. But we've had worse."

And then, finally, *finally,* he kissed me. Gentle at first, as though testing whether I'd break, then deeper, his hand still cupping my cheek. Evie gave a disgruntled huff from my lap, but I ignored her. The clinic could be burning down, and I would not care.

When we pulled apart, I felt a sappy smile stretch from cheek to cheek.

"Worth the wait?" Nick asked, brushing his thumb across my cheek.

"Oh yeah," I said. "But next time, maybe without the near-death experience."

"No promises." He leaned in and kissed me again.

The "Closed for mild trauma" sign on the clinic's front door had worked surprisingly well. I'd only had to turn away one client who claimed their poodle's diarrhea was an emergency. The rest of the week, I'd spent catching up on sleep, fielding calls from curious locals, and watching Evie strut around the house like she expected a medal of valor. Honestly, I was considering it.

The police had recovered Trudy's—and only Trudy's—fingerprints on the suicide note, as well as the empty bottle of phenobarbital, and Mrs. B's coffee thermos.

When I opened the clinic Monday morning, a "Welcome Back, Hero" banner hung over the front desk. I had no idea who put it there, but it had suspiciously neat handwriting. Probably Tess. She'd always had a flair for the dramatic, as evidenced by the numerous phone calls and visits to get all the juicy details of the "fateful night."

Speaking of drama, the entire town had exploded with gossip. By Wednesday, three people claimed to have seen Trudy wandering the fairgrounds "with a crazed look in her eye," and someone said they overheard her muttering about poisons in the concession stand line. I kind of doubted that last claim. Nick would have noticed.

Of course, none of them had said anything *before* she held me at gunpoint. But I supposed hindsight was a powerful thing.

I was sipping coffee when Nick appeared in the doorway, holding a bakery bag in one hand and a ribbon in the other.

"You're just in time," I said. "I was about to see if Evie wanted to open her fan mail."

He set the bag down and held up the ribbon. "She won this. Posthumously, in Mildred's name. The club wanted to honor her for bravery and . . . I quote . . . 'ferocious loyalty beyond her weight class.'"

I laughed. "Evie will be insufferable."

"She already is. But she deserves it." He reached

into the bakery bag and pulled out two cinnamon rolls the size of hubcaps. "Also, I come bearing carbs."

"You're the real hero."

We sat at the table in the break room, Evie between us, gnawing on a celebratory chew toy shaped like a villain. I took a bite of cinnamon roll and moaned.

"Okay, I take it back," I said. "*This* is the best kiss I've had all week."

Nick raised an eyebrow. "I'm wounded."

I licked frosting off my finger. "Sorry. You're second. Unless you brought coffee, in which case we might have a tie."

He pulled out a thermos. "Am I back to the first again?"

I smiled. "Always."

We ate in comfortable silence for a few minutes, the worst behind us, the future finally beginning to feel like a place I might want to live in again.

"Hey," Nick said, his tone shifting. "You really okay? For real?"

I looked around the clinic. At the cabinets where the drugs were locked tightly. At the spot on the floor where I'd bashed Trudy's head with the fire extinguisher. (She suffered a mild concussion and numerous bite wounds to her ankle, but was otherwise fine.) At Evie's wagging tail. At Nick.

And I realized I really was okay.

"Yeah," I said.

Nick nodded. "You know, I meant what I said. You were incredible."

"Thanks. Though I'd really like my next act of courage to involve something less... felony-involving."

"You could try dating me."

I chuckled. "Wow. That was smooth."

"I've been practicing."

I grinned. "Does this mean I've obtained official girlfriend status?"

"Yeah, I guess it does."

Epilogue

Three weeks later, the community dog show was back in full swing, complete with glittery leashes, bedazzled blazers, and enough sequins to blind a referee. I was there not as a vet this time, but as a proud dog mom and—though I was still wrapping my head around it—someone's girlfriend. Nick had shown up that morning with collapsible camp chairs, bottles of water, and a "Team Evie" T-shirt, which he claimed was iconic.

One woman stopped me on our way into the fairgrounds. "Is that *the* Evie?" she asked, her voice reverent.

"The one and only."

"She bit someone, didn't she?"

"Just the once. She was saving my life."

"Oh, bless her heart." The woman leaned down to scratch Evie behind the ears. "I hope you give her bacon every morning."

"Bacon is bad for dogs," I said. "But she gets the gourmet dog food in the tiny, expensive tins."

Evie sneezed, which I took as agreement.

Nick threw an arm around my shoulders. "You know you're kind of a legend now, right?"

"I don't want to be a legend. I just want a normal life where no one gets murdered around me and no one points a gun at me."

He tilted his head. "Fair. But if that *does* happen again, I assume Evie will handle it while you smack someone with a fire extinguisher."

"Once is enough, thank you."

A man running toward us caught my eye. Officer Lang. I thought—I'd hoped—I'd seen the last of him. I let out a groan.

"Dr. Dixon!"

I gritted my teeth. "Officer Lang. If you're here to keep an eye on me, I assure you I have no intention of poisoning anyone today."

"Funny," he replied without laughing. "Actually, I came to congratulate you. And to bring you something."

I looked down and noticed he held a crate in his hand. My inner Spidey senses began to tingle. "That better not be—"

"Bentley. Trudy asked if you'd take him. She doesn't have anybody else to give him to, and she knows you'll take good care of him."

My jaw dropped. "Seriously? The woman tries to kill me, then expects me to take care of her dog?"

Nick chuckled. "If you keep going at this rate, people are going to start calling you the crazy Chihuahua lady."

I shook my head and flattened my lips. "No, nope, absolutely not."

Lang brought the cage up to my eye level, and I

stood nose to nose with the beautiful tan Chihuahua with caramel-colored eyes. My heart melted.

"Fine," I snapped. "But this is the last one." After all, it wasn't Bentley's fault his owner was incarcerated for murder.

Lang handed the crate off to Nick. "Thanks, I'm sure Trudy will feel a lot better."

"Well, her peace of mind has certainly been my number one priority," I muttered, glancing at Nick. His eyes danced with amusement. "What? I couldn't just let a special-needs dog go to the shelter."

"No, of course not. But we'd better hurry. The opening ceremony is about to start."

The show kicked off with a grand ceremony honoring Mildred and Evie. Mr. Wigglesworth, of all people, offered a fitting tribute to the late Mrs. Blankenship and her extraordinary dog. I pasted on a smile and took the high road. After a while, I tuned him out while he pontificated on and on about Mildred Blankenship's contributions to the show dog world. Finally, he presented Evie with a ribbon "for exemplary obedience, bravery, and panache." I wasn't entirely sure what category that fell under, but we'd take it.

As we walked off the field, applause broke out. My fifteen minutes of fame felt good.

"Dr. Dixon, wait!"

We turned to see Mr. Wigglesworth trotting toward us. He wiped perspiration from his forehead as though he'd sprinted a hundred yards instead of ten. Reaching into his pocket, he pulled out an envelope.

"I forgot to give you this."

"What is it?" I asked, accepting the envelope from him.

"It's your fee for veterinary services at the dog show a few weeks ago. I was holding on to it until you were cleared of Mrs. Blankenship's murder."

"Gee, thanks," I muttered. I guess convicted felons didn't get paid for services rendered.

"And, I was wondering. Dr. Collins is thinking about retiring as the show veterinarian. Would you be interested in the position?"

I exchanged glances with Nick. "Uh, thanks, but I don't think so. Too much drama for me."

"All right, but if you change your mind—"

"I'll be sure to let you know." *As if.*

He walked away, his chest puffed out with importance. I slipped a finger under the envelope flap and took out a check for $1000. *$1000!*

"Nick!" I grasped his arm. "Look how much they paid me."

Nick's eyes grew wide. "Holy cow, that's a lot of money for one day's work."

"Now I can pay Joanna for Corky."

I watched Mr. Wigglesworth's retreating back. "Oh, Mr. Wigglesworth," I called, racing after him. "Wait!"

THANK YOU, DEAR READER

If you enjoyed reading this book, the best thing you can do to help the author is to tell others about it. Ellen would also greatly appreciate your rating her book and leaving a brief review at amazon.com and goodreads.com. Simply type in the name of the book and the author. When the website comes up, click on the picture of the book, scroll down, and there will be a button to click to leave a rating and a review. A review doesn't have to be long—a sentence or two telling what you liked about the book. Was it interesting, humorous, informative, thought-provoking, etc.? Thank you so much for your support.

Ellen would love for you to visit her website: https://ellenfannonauthor.com and subscribe to follow her weekly blog, *Good for a Laugh.*

Follow Ellen on Facebook:
https://www.facebook.com/ellenfannonauthor

The author with Chihuahuas, Fritz and Frannie

SAVE THE DATE

2022 Christian Indie Award Winner

What if you were given the chance to rekindle the flame with your first love? What happened to all those girls who were mean to you in school? Should Hannah Jensen take the chance of attending her high school reunion to find out?

Hannah hasn't been back to her hometown in twenty-five years. Now a widow raising a teenaged daughter, she has the opportunity to go home for her twenty-fifth high school reunion. The invitation to the reunion stirs up a lot of old memories at the same time she is dealing with loneliness, the challenges of single-parenting a teenager, people who want to "set her up" with eligible men, her own insecurities, and her eccentric family.

The story interweaves the present with scenes from Hannah's past and her fantasy of "happily ever after" with her high school boyfriend in a humorous and entertaining manner. Her feelings from being "shunned" by the cool kids resurface as she reflects back on her time as a teenager. There are several roadblocks on Hannah's journey from a teenager through her present. The growing pains and amusing situations in which she finds herself are ones to which we all can relate. As she walks the path of self-discovery, she also discovers the most important life lesson of all–her relationship to God.

<u>DON'T BITE THE DOCTOR</u>

Real doctors treat more than one species. At least that's what veterinarian, Jill Bennet tells herself. On any given day, she may find herself doctoring dogs, cats, bunnies, birds, horses, pigs, or any other furry or feathered patient who crosses her path—striving daily to deliver compassion and competence to all God's creatures, in accordance with Colossians 3:23. Now, with over forty years of practice under her belt, Jill reflects back to her time as a new, young veterinarian in the early eighties—a time when women veterinarians were just beginning to become a presence among the previously male-dominated profession. Out in the real world, Jill finds herself in situations never covered in veterinary school. It is a journey of learning and laughter, as Jill contends with a variety of animal patients and their eclectic humans attached to the other end of the leash (and the checkbook), as well as less-than-helpful co-workers. Interwoven into this mix of new experiences is her budding romance with the owner of the sock-eating Labrador Retriever. *Don't Bite the Doctor* promises to bring smiles and tears to anyone who has ever been owned by an animal.

OTHER PEOPLE's CHILDREN

As a mid-thirties childless woman, Robin has all the answers on proper parenting. It doesn't take long, however, for Robin to realize that her perfect parenting ideas and reality often collide – the result being an amusing journey of finding out that God, indeed, has a sense of humor. As she deals with the baggage, idiosyncrasies, unique personalities, and special gifts of each child that crosses her path, she finds that there is no "one-size fits all" to parenting. However, in spite of the challenges she and her husband face, they are determined to become the children's strongest advocates in a flawed system that often fails the very victims it is designed to protect. The journey is often heartbreaking and frustrating, but these foster parents are firmly resolved that for whatever time they have children in their care, the children will know they are safe, protected, and loved by God, as well as by their foster parents.

HONOR THY FATHER EPISODE ONE

HONOR THY FATHER EPISODE TWO

Why should Adam's daughters, with whom he hasn't had contact for twenty-five years, honor him now when he needs a life-saving bone marrow transplant? Why should his son, who was kicked out of the house, honor his father? Is there any hope of reconciliation when twenty-five years of anger, bitterness, and divergent pathways have led family members down different roads of life? *Honor Thy Father* is the compelling story of loss and redemption and how God can turn tragedy into triumph.

How does a family survive after being torn apart? Adam Wallace copes with the heartbreaking loss of his wife and daughters by immersing himself in his work. Charlotte withdraws from everyone and everything around her. Dana, living a life of privilege, does not even realize her loss. Katrina copes by trying to make everyone else happy. Scott copes by rebellion. Ultimately, they all come to realize that God can work through every situation to make beauty out of ashes.

LOVE IN THE WIND

Book 1 in the Love in the Wind Series

2024 Living Water Award Winner

Wyoming rancher, Ben Parish, is struggling to keep his ranch afloat. Veterinarian, Darcy Fuller has moved to Wyoming to start a new life but is struggling to become established in a new area. Both have been badly burned by past relationships and are not looking to become involved in another. When their paths cross, Darcy has an idea to bring extra income to the ranch, as well as provide her with an outlet for her passion for working with horses. But can their growing attraction coexist with a business partnership?

FALLING FOR A COWBOY

Book 2 in the Love in the Wind Series

Biology professor, Kendra Clark, is an independent, competent, intelligent woman of faith—that is, until she is around cowboy, Ricky Gaither. Then she becomes a babbling klutz. For his part, Ricky doesn't have much use for intellectuals or God. But when they keep running into each other, they can't deny their growing attraction. Can a relationship work between two people who seem to have nothing in common? Or does the secret Ricky harbors make them more alike than Kendra realizes? And will that secret derail any hope for a relationship?

LOVE'S TRAIL OF REDEMPTION
Book 3 in the Love in the Wind Series
Cam Ellis and Olivia Anderson have worked at Whispering Winds Ranch for two years without paying much attention to each other—until suddenly, things change. They are a perfect match in every way, except for the one challenge neither of them expected to enter their lives.

Will an event from Cam's past hold him hostage to moving forward, or can he overcome his deepest fear to risk everything for love?

www.ingramcontent.com/pod-product-compliance
Lightning Source LLC
Chambersburg PA
CBHW060305310726
48976CB00007B/2224